STR

'Hold on!' Pete shouted, f

being shot out from und wrestling with the steering wheel, the explosive charge on the side of the van detonated with so much force that the entire vehicle was jolted upward and Pete had only two flat tyres making contact with the ground. Joe dropped his gun and braced himself in his seat and the van lunged off the road. Carried along by its reckless momentum, the van ploughed through a stack of packing crates and rolled up a loading ramp before flipping onto its side in front of a warehouse storage dock. Even as the van was screeching to a metal-grinding halt, another explosion ripped away the rear doors as if they were petals on a wilting flower . . .

STREET HAWK

Based on the Universal television series 'Street Hawk'
Created by Robert Wolterstorff & Paul M. Belous and
Bruce Lansbury
Adapted from the episode 'Street Hawk'
Written by Robert Wolterstorff & Paul M. Belous

A novel by
JACK ROBERTS

A TARGET BOOK
published by
the Paperback Division of
W. H. ALLEN & Co. PLC

A Target Book
Published in 1985
by the Paperback Division of
W. H. Allen & Co. PLC
44 Hill Street, London W1X 8LB

Printed and bound in Great Britain by
Anchor Brendon Ltd, Tiptree, Essex

ISBN 0 426 20185 X

ONE

There was a first-stage smog alert in the Los Angeles basin, and the sun rose bleakly through tarnished air to begin its trek across the Sunday sky. It was shortly after dawn and the city's warehouse district was quiet. Long shadows stretched out from the bases of tall brick buildings, casting a relative darkness across vacant parking lots and still streets. A slight breeze jostled scraps of litter in the gutters, and a few transients staggered along cracked sidewalks, having been roused from their wine-soaked dreams by rays of sun that crept into the niches where they had crawled off to sleep the night before. When a black and white police van suddenly rolled into view down the deserted street, the bedraggled men shuffled hastily to the cover of doorways and side alleys, not wishing to be hauled into the station on another count of vagrancy. Their concern was unnecessary, however, because the officers in the van were tending to matters of higher consequence than cracking down on loitering misfits.

'"He was accused by critics of casting his sculpture 'Age of Bronze' from a model instead of actually sculpting the work."' A grey-haired officer grinned as he looked up from the question card and took a sip of coffee from his thermos. He was riding shotgun, and his partner, a man half his age, bit his lower lip as he drove through the next intersection and contemplated the question.

'Beats me,' the younger man said, shaking his head. 'Michaelangelo?'

'Hah! Not even close!' his partner chortled. 'It was Rodin. I tell ya, Pete, you're gonna have to bone up on the arts if you expect to win anything on that game show. Let's try another one...'

Pete noticed one of the vagrants ducking underneath a stone staircase in front of a boarded-up factory, but didn't bother mentioning it to his partner. Instead, he grabbed his own cup from the dashboard and held it out for the other man to fill, saying, 'I think maybe I'll just look around for a show that has only sports questions.'

'You find me a show that has just sports questions and even *I'll* try out for it...'

As the older officer flipped to another question card and continued quizzing his partner, Pete kept driving down the abandoned side streets toward the Harbor Freeway. The Harbor would take them all the way to San Pedro, where they would turn over the cargo in the back of their van to a waiting Coast Guard crew that would, in turn, dispose of the material far out in the depths of the Pacific. The vehicle was still a few miles away from the Freeway entrance when a pickup truck appeared out of a back alley and began to follow them. The truck was a gleaming black, its body elevated above the chassis to give ample room for the monstrous balloon tyres that held it to the road. With windows tinted a shade of dark grey, it was impossible to see who was behind the wheel as it sped along the street like a panther in search of prey – the police van that headed down the road in front of it.

'"Artist famous for his paintings of limp watches."'

'Dali,' Pete answered between sips of coffee. 'Am I right?'

His partner checked on the back of the question card and nodded. 'Hey, how about that? Keep it up, Pete, and before you know it –'

'Just a sec, Joe,' Pete interrupted, checking his rear-view mirror. 'We got company...'

Joe craned his neck to look back, catching a partial view of the approaching truck. 'Hmm, that bugger's a long way from the sand dunes.'

'Think we oughta call it in?' Pete asked, reaching for the microphone of his police radio.

'Naw, not yet. Let's just keep an eye on it.' Joe unsnapped the flap on his holster and patted the butt of his service revolver. 'If there're any problems, we can handle 'em . . .'

Pete eased down on the accelerator and the van sped down a stretch of straightaway next to several canneries and a packing house, all closed for the weekend. The pickup kept pace with the van, and its rear doors opened eerily behind it. Like a thick, metallic tongue, a ramp slowly angled down from inside the truck, coming within less than a foot of making contact with the street. A boisterous roar sounded from within the shelled enclosure, and soon a pair of light-weight motorcross dirt bikes were backing down the ramp. Riding the machines were helmeted men in red leather suits with padded yellow vests that gave them a futuristic appearance. With consummate skill, the two riders worked their throttles so that when the bikes cleared the ramp and landed on the asphalt of the street, they were able to maintain control and balance. Following what was obviously a well-planned manoeuvre, the pickup slowed down and allowed the bikers to race past it on either side and take up positions close behind the police van.

'Hey, did you just see what I saw?' Joe gasped, straining to catch sight of the bikers in the side-view mirror. They were riding too close to the van to be seen, but Joe was able to spot the pickup as it turned off into a side street.

As Pete grabbed the radio microphone, he nodded at his partner. 'Yeah, and I don't like it. I'm calling in some backup . . .'

While a report was hastily being relayed to the dispatcher at the downtown police station, the two men on the motorcycles carried out the next phase of their well-choreographed assault on the police van. The rider on the right revved his engine until he was within inches of the rear of the van, then held his speed as he leaned forward and quickly pressed a plastic explosive to the back door of the police vehicle. Then he sat back and guided his cycle over to one side before speeding forward and attaching a second charge to the side door of the van.

'What the hell!!' Joe saw the saboteur riding alongside him and grabbed for his gun as he started rolling down the window. He told Pete, 'Tell 'em they're definitely trying to make a hit on us . . .'

As Pete passed along the message over the radio, he noticed the second cyclist approaching from his side of the van. Keeping his right hand on the throttle, the rider raised his other arm and pointed at the front tyre of the van. Mounted on the rider's wrist was a sophisticated miniature cannon, which fired an explosive-tipped dart at the wheel, ripping through rubber and steel-belting. The van immediately began to swerve sharply to one side, jarring Joe just as the officer was about to fire a shot at his pursuer. Pete was forced to drop the microphone and grab at the steering wheel with both hands in a desperate effort to keep the van from veering out of control. In countering the skidding of the van, he sent Joe leaning sharply back toward him and the older officer's potshot at the biker on the right scarred the side of a nearby building.

'Hold on!' Pete shouted, feeling yet another of the van's tyres being shot out from under him. As he continued wrestling with the steering wheel, the explosive charge on the side of the van detonated with so much force that the entire vehicle was jolted upward and Pete had only two flat tyres making contact with the ground. Joe dropped his gun and braced himself in his seat as the quiz cards flew off his lap and the van lunged off the road. Carried along by its reckless momentum, the van ploughed through a stack of packing crates and rolled up a loading ramp before flipping onto its side in front of a warehouse storage dock. Even as the van was screeching to a metal-grinding halt, another explosion ripped away the rear doors as if they were petals on a wilting flower.

Inside the ravaged van, Pete slumped motionlessly against his door, blood trickling from a brutal gash on his forehead. He was unconscious, but breathing. Joe had survived the wreck, too, and had been thrown halfway out of the window he'd rolled down prior to the first explosion. He groaned and stirred as the two bikers circled around their downed prey. One of the bikers rode over and gave Joe a sharp karate chop to the back of the head, knocking him out. The other man idled his bike behind the van and dismounted, unslinging a set of leather saddlebags from behind his seat and disappearing inside the disabled vehicle. Scattered about the interior of the van were numerous brick-sized plastic bags filled with an unmistakable white powder. The man quickly stuffed the bags into the large pockets of the leather carrier, then climbed back out and flashed a signal to his partner.

The howl of sirens cut through the morning air as a pair of speeding police cruisers raced toward the scene. The biker with the saddlebags hurriedly fastened his load back onto his machine, then joined his partner in roaring off down the street. The arriving patrol officers quickly assessed the situation and followed in pursuit of the fleeing bikers. Off in the distance, the wail of other sirens announced that an ambulance had been summoned to tend to the officers in the crashed van.

The chase wound through the warehouse district, with the bikers taking advantage of their smaller vehicles to manoeuvre through openings unreachable by the bulkier patrol cars. The police were able to remain within sight of the two-wheelers, however, and when a number of other cruisers responded to an all-points bulletin and converged upon the scene, they were able to narrow down the possible escape options. The bikers found themselves having to constantly cut down alleys and take to the sidewalk to avoid capture, and while racing through the back lot of a produce wholesaler, there was almost a head-on collision between a pair of patrol cars and both cycles. The bikers managed to narrowly avert the collision, however, and whisk through a side gate to a section of rail yard.

By the time the police were able to gain access to the yard, the bikers had stretched out the distance between them, and when they rounded a corner at the end of the yard, they were gone from view for the first time since the chase had begun. The pursuing vehicles sped to close the distance and screeched around the corner, then braked to a sudden halt. The disbelieving officers stared at the dead end in front of them. There was a storm grating and concrete walls covered with graffiti and outdated concert posters, but no trace of the villains or their motorcycles.

One of the officers slowly got out of his car and scratched

his head in wonder.

'Man, oh man,' he grumbled under his breath. 'The chief's not gonna like this . . .'

TWO

'How the hell could two motorcycle thieves and fifty pounds of cocaine disappear into thin air?!!'

Police Commander Leo Altobelli was only a year away from drawing a full pension, and this wasn't the kind of aggravation he needed to see him through his final year. What with his bleeding ulcer and chronic indigestion, he figured there was no one in his entire division with a lousier plumbing system, and news of this morning's heist had set his guts churning with their usual agonizing zeal. He'd been on the case for less than an hour and he was already halfway through a fresh pack of antacid tablets. As he popped another dose into his mouth, he paced before the twisted bulk of the damaged van, watching a burly, bearded mechanic rig a towing bar to the back bumper. Altobelli was in his early fifties, with short-cropped hair flecked with grey. He wore a tailored brown suit, but the collar of his dress shirt was loose and the knot of his tie hung well below the top button. Once he'd chewed down the antacid, he turned on the handful of officers standing around him.

'I asked a question, dammit!' Altobelli picked up one of the quiz cards and pretended to be reading from it. '"Two dirt bikers blow up a police van like it was a toy, then run off with fifty pounds of confiscated cocaine and disappear into thin air when four patrol cruisers are closing in on them for certain arrest." Now, for fifty points and the championship... *How*?!!'

The other officers shrugged and looked away, avoiding Altobelli's withering gaze. A few yards away, paramedics finished loading the two wounded officers into the back of their ambulance, then started up their sirens as they headed off for the nearest hospital.

'Well?' Altobelli raged. 'Nobody have any bright answers around here? Nobody wants to take Officer Jenkins' place on the game show next week? How'd they do it? I want to know!'

'Mirrors,' the mechanic wheezed as he finished linking the tow bar to the fender and started hoisting up the van with the power winch on his tow truck. 'Coulda been mirrors.'

'What are you talking about?'

The mechanic waited until he'd managed to raise the van and tip it rightside up, then turned off his winch and rubbed his palms together as he explained, 'I seen it in Vegas, chief. Siegfried and Roy . . . they made a whole jet disappear, right up there on the stage. And they done it with mirrors!'

'Terrific.' Altobelli glared at the twisted frame of the police van and shook his head with disgust. 'Do me a favour and make this thing disappear! Get it outta my sight before it makes me sick!'

'You got it.'

As the mechanic double-checked his connections, Altobelli strode past the officers and pointed to two of them, declaring, 'I want a full report on this on my desk by noon. And I want those bikers tracked down and in jail by midnight or you're all gonna be tryin' out for game shows to make ends meet!'

Even on Sunday mornings, news had a way of travelling fast, and no less than five different media vehicles had descended upon the robbery scene in the past hour. The police had cordoned off the area around the van, but a drove of photographers and reporters lingered in the background, cameras running as representatives from various stations hustled to get the inside story on what had happened. One reporter had managed to latch onto the police department's Public Relations director, Sandy McCoy, a sharp-dressing young woman who projected an exterior calm even in the face of this image-souring development.

'Come on, Sandy,' the reporter prodded, walking beside the woman as she headed back to her car. 'You used to be a reporter. You know the spot I'm in. Come on, give me something . . . anything.'

Sandy stopped once she reached her car and faced the reporter squarely. 'Larry, I already told you all I intend to. We're withholding comment until after the investigation. It would be premature to make any statements before all the facts are in.'

'You expect me to go on the air with that?' Larry laughed bitterly. 'Hey, they won't cut away to me unless I've got something better than that. I need some colour. I need a draw.'

'Then maybe you should check around for a girl in a bikini, Larry.' Sandy opened her car door and slid in behind the wheel. 'Interview her for her reaction.'

'Very funny.' Larry stood aside as Sandy backed out of her parking space and drove slowly over to where Commander Altobelli was checking out the interior of the bombed van along with Bernie Goldberg, the division's ace lab man. Bernie was in his late thirties, with a thick beard offsetting his retreating hairline. He was wearing his everpresent white lab coat.

'Is there anything else I can do, commander?' Sandy called out.

'You by any chance goin' to the store on your way back to the station?' Altobelli asked. When Sandy nodded, he said, 'Pick me up another bottle of Pepto Bismol. I gotta feeling I'm gonna be ready for a good stiff drink when I get back.'

'Sure thing.'

When he turned his attention back to the van, Altobelli noticed Bernie transferring something into a clear plastic bag. 'Hey, you got something there, Bernie?'

'Yeah...' Bernie's lips curled, tipping off a smile as he looked away from his boss and said, 'I think it's part of a mirror...'

'Oh, that's rich, pal,' Altobelli snarled. 'Bernie, you're a laugh a lifetime.'

Before she drove off, Sandy hesitated, then cleared her throat and told Altobelli, 'I hate to be the one to say it, commander, but it might be a good idea for you to give a statement to the press so they'll go home. It doesn't have to be...'

'No way!' Altobelli shook his head firmly as he started taking long strides toward a helicopter that was waiting for him at the back corner of the parking lot. 'I'm not talking to 'em, and that's final!!'

'Remember the last time we got hit during a drug transport?' Sandy told him. 'The papers crucified us, and we didn't fare that well on the tube, either.'

'They'll crucify us anyway,' Altobelli speculated. 'Why should I make their job easier for them?'

Sandy sighed with frustration as she watched the man duck low and climb into the cockpit of the helicopter, taking a seat next to the pilot. 'That's why I like working with you so much, commander,' she shouted. 'You're so damn image-conscious!'

'Get me outta here,' Altobelli told the pilot as he strapped himself in his seat and stared ruefully at the phalanx of cameramen and reporters recording the towing of the disabled van away from the scene. A few reporters and photographers managed to sneak around the cordon and move in closer for some better shots. The commander shook an angry fist at them and the officers who were trying to herd the media back behind police lines. 'I don't get it,' he complained, more to himself than to the pilot. 'We oughta have a good dozen men down there moppin' up, and instead there's only five. Where the hell *is* everybody . . . ?'

THREE

In San Pedro, less than a couple of miles from where the police van had been scheduled to deliver its supply of confiscated cocaine, it looked as if half of the city's police force had gathered in one of the loading yards adjacent to Los Angeles harbour. Four police cruisers were parked side by side in the middle of a clearing, while other black and white four-wheelers rested in the background along with a handful of patrol motorcycles. While two groups of officers positioned slanting ramps on either side of the four cruisers, a dozen other men were gathered around patrolman Marty Walsh, a swaggering, good-looking young man with a fistful of dollars and the baiting grin of a carnival barker holding court at his favourite game booth.

'Four to one!?' he cried out with disbelief at the officer closest to him. 'Farnsworth, you gotta be kidding! Mach is risking his life here, for crying out loud! I mean, take a good look at that setup over there, wouldya? My man's gonna jump four squad cars in a police hog. We're talking Evil Knievel stuff here, not some chintzy kid's game. Four to one? Sheesh, you maybe want him to ride backwards and wear a blindfold, too?'

Farnsworth rolled his eyes and ran his fingers through his hair. 'Cut the hustle, Walsh,' he chided. 'Your partner's good at this stuff and you know it. Quit playing us for suckers!'

Walsh fanned his bets in Farnsworth's face. 'Hey, this is from folks that have a proper appreciation of the true danger Mach's facing. Two to one is the best I can give you. Double your money. Hell, you can't get those kinda odds at the track!

Now put up or shut up, 'cause it's gettin' close to blast-off time.'

Farnsworth's pockets were bulging with bucks he'd pooled together from officers who weren't able to make it to the harbour. He patted down the money to make sure it was still there, then sighed, 'I can't bet on those odds without clearing it first.'

Walsh grinned and patted Farnsworth on the shoulder. 'Well, clear away, pal.' Checking his watch, he added, 'You've got four minutes before all bets are closed!'

As Walsh turned his attention to other officers looking to place wagers, Farnsworth retreated to his patrol car and grabbed the radio mike.

'All units. Odds information on the first annual harbour jump...'

'... now going off at two to one... respond.'

Commander Altobelli frowned as he overheard the dispatch. He turned to the chopper pilot and asked, 'What the hell is the first annual harbour jump?'

The pilot grinned stiffly and shook his head. 'Beats me, commander.'

They were flying over the heart of the downtown area, heading for division headquarters. The sun was burning through the morning haze, but a layer of smog still muted the air. Over the radio, Altobelli heard a sputter of affirmatives crackle.

'I'm in, Farny.'

'Tobey here. I'll got for it.'

'Double my bet.'

As he peeled the wrapper off another antacid, Altobelli told the pilot, 'I think we'll make a little detour...'

Officer Farnsworth counted out a majority of his bills and handed them over to Marty Walsh. 'I got a few dropouts, and I still say two to one's not good enough...'

'Yeah yeah yeah.' Marty licked his thumb and quickly double-checked the bills, then called out to the other officers, 'Anybody else have some money they want to get rid of?'

'That's everybody, Walsh,' Farnsworth said. 'Now where's Mach?'

'Yeah,' another officer muttered. 'Bring on the legend.'

Marty pocketed the bets and waded through his peers to a portable cassette player perched on the hood of a patrol car. As he pushed the play button, he shouted, 'Okay, it's showtime!'

For such a small piece of equipment, the cassette player packed a lot of audio wallop, filling the harbour lot with the orchestrated frenzy of Rossini's 'William Tell Overture'. On cue with the swelling surge of music, a throaty roar sounded from one of the warehouses and motorcycle cop Jesse Mach raced out into view astride his stock police Kawasaki. He was in uniform, but for today's performance he had forsaken his regulation helmet for a stars-and-stripes motorcross headpiece, beneath which he wore a pair of World War I aviator goggles. To round out the theatrical embellishments, a long red cape trailed from his neck, unfurling and snapping behind him as he rode past the gathered officers, who greeted him with a chorus of jeers and cheers. He acknowledged the ovation with a wave of his hand, then veered toward the closest ramp and guided the bike halfway up it before braking. For a moment, he stayed in place, grinning back at his fellow officers. Then he shifted to neutral and rolled back down the ramp before riding in a slow, lazy circle around the clearing, letting the tension build.

Two hundred feet away, an uninvited spectator was viewing the proceedings through the eyepiece of a portable video camera. Norman Tuttle was a clerkish-looking man in his late thirties, with dark, curly hair framing his prominent forehead and slightly freckled features. He wore horn-rimmed glasses and a corduroy sports jacket over a checked shirt. There was a 'nebbish' quality about him, but the intelligence stored in his intent gaze suggested that he didn't project himself as the glamorous type because he preferred to be judged on the merits of his mind. As such, the sight of the costumed daredevil jockeying the throttle of the Kawasaki down in the clearing was particularly disturbing.

'They can't be serious,' he grumbled to himself as he adjusted the focus for a clearer view of Mach. 'This guy belongs in a comic book, not on my project. There has to be a mistake somewhere.'

Norman was crouched on the stairway of a fire escape clinging to the side of an old warehouse. From his perspective, he had a clear view of the four squad cars parked between the jumping ramps, and when he guessed that Mach was ready to follow through with the challenge, he took a deep breath and started filming.

'I ought to be taping this for the six o'clock news,' he murmured, imagining the headlines: 'Hotdog Bike Cop Kills Self Pulling Stupid Stunt . . .'

Jesse Mach didn't consider the stunt to be stupid. Ill-advised, yes. Dangerous, maybe. He'd spent almost half of his twenty-five years risking life and limb in the pursuit of two-wheeled pleasure, and on several occasions he'd made longer jumps than the one he was proposing to make today. But he'd never gone this airborne on a bike the size of the Kawasaki now rumbling between his knees.

'Why do I listen to you, Marty?' he wondered to himself as he stared at the ramp and revved the throttle while holding the clutch open. Out of the corner of his eye he saw his partner waving at him.

'Hey, hurry it up before the music's over!' Walsh shouted to him.

Jesse sighed and gave Marty a thumbs-up signal, then braced himself for the inevitable. He wasn't the least bit concerned about how much money Marty had gotten the others to lay down. His full concentration was now on the ramp and the controls of his bike. If he was going to pull this off, he couldn't afford any distractions.

'Five . . . four . . .' he muttered, checking his RPMs as he gave the engine more gas.

'Three . . . two . . .' His gloved fingers slowly began to ease up on the clutch handle.

'One . . . blast-off!'

With a piercing squeal, the Kawasaki plunged forward.

Jesse clung to the bike, opening up the throttle all the way as he adjusted his weight in preparation for the jump. The asphalt below became a blur as he hurtled past the officers. He gauged the middle of the ramp and felt his stomach rise as the bike hit the incline and took to the air. Time seemed to bog down in a twilight zone of slow motion as he leaned forward, catching a glimpse of the patrol cars he was flying over. He had pulled up on the front end of the bike, and a jolt of terror coursed through him as he felt a momentary nudge against his rear tyre. He'd lightly clipped the light fixture atop the last car, but not enough to throw the bike off balance. With sure precision, he landed on the far ramp, back end first, then touhed down the front tyre and cleared the ramp without losing control of the cycle.

'All right!!!' Marty led the cheers of those who had bet in Mach's favour. Farnsworth and the other officers groaned and otherwise hid their secret relief that Mach hadn't killed himself making the jump.

'Damn fool. I can't believe he actually went through with it,' Farnsworth muttered.

'Cursed be thou of little faith!' Marty taunted as he ran over to where Jesse had brought the Kawasaki to a stop in front of the other police choppers. Turning his back to the other officers, Marty hissed, 'What were you trying to do out there, Jesse? You practically gave me a heart attack!'

Jesse pulled off his helmet and lowered the goggles as he shook his hair loose. 'Aw, were you worried about me, Marty?' he smirked.

'Do you know how much money we had riding on this?' Marty wailed. 'Look... next time don't cut it so close, okay? Or if you're gonna, let me know so I can bet against you!'

Jesse continued straddling his bike as he watched Marty head back to the others, churning out the bravado. 'Okay, gentlemen. It's payday!'

There was a sudden disruption as the airspace above the harbour lot was invaded by a low-banking police chopper.

'Altobelli!' Farnsworth shrieked, sounding the alarm as he rushed toward his patrol car. The rest of the men in blue fell into a similar state of panic, scattering in all directions. Soon the area was filled with the mad flight of screeching patrol cars and racing motorcycles.

'Stop! Hold it!' Marty shouted at his fleeing counterparts. 'Get back here with our money!'

'What a guy,' Jesse said, watching his friend chase after the patrol car that was rolling away with the cassette deck still resting on its hood. Marty was barely able to snatch the player before it toppled to the asphalt.

'I'll get you for that, Farnsworth!' Marty vowed. 'And I'm gonna charge interest on all the bets that aren't paid off by the end of the day!'

'Forget the money,' Jesse yelled as he rode over to Marty's side. 'Let's get out of here before we end up in big trouble.'

Shielding his face like a convicted felon avoiding the press, Marty snuck a quick glance at the descending helicopter, then reluctantly hopped on the back of Jesse's cycle. Jesse gave the Kawasaki some gas and headed for the nearby warehouses.

'I don't believe this!' Altobelli roared as he looked down at the mass exodus of his charges. 'Crime's up five percent in my division and I bust my own men for illegal gambling! Heads are gonna roll!'

The pilot continued to lower the helicopter as he asked the commander, 'What do you want me to do?'

'I want *them*!' Altobelli declared, pointing at Mach and Walsh.

'Who?'

'Captain America and Bucky . . .'

Norman Tuttle watched the disruption in the lot with mixed emotions. Having witnessed and filmed Mach's successful jump, he had to grudgingly admit that the man was qualified to join his project, but he also knew that the odds on the two of them being compatible seemed next to nil. When he saw the police chopper pursuing Mach and Walsh toward the warehouses, he found himself hoping that both officers would have the book thrown at them.

'They can't stick him with me if he's in jail,' Norman mused as he dismantled his video gear and began putting it back in his leather carrying case. Once he had finished the task, he stole carefully down the fire escape to the first floor, where he entered the warehouse and emerged behind the building. His car was parked there, and after putting the camera equipment in the trunk, he got in behind the wheel and drove off.

On the side of the vehicle was an official-looking decal declaring that Norman Tuttle was affiliated with the Federal Institute of Law Enforcement Technological Development.

'Tuttle here,' Norman reported over a shortwave radio as he made his way back to the Harbour Freeway. 'I've got the footage you're looking for, but it might be beside the point now...'

'How's that?' came the reply over the radio speakers.

'I'll explain when I get there...'

Jesse parked the Kawasaki in the dark shadows of the warehouse interior, then he and Marty dismounted and crouched behind a stack of oil drums. As they stared out at the gaping entrance to the warehouse, Marty speculated, 'You think he made us?'

Jesse shook his head. 'Nah. No way.'

The words were barely out of Jesse's mouth when the police 'copter dropped into view before the opening and Altobelli's voice assaulted them through an electronic bullhorn.

'Mach, I want you and Walsh in my office in twenty minutes!'

The helicopter pulled away from the entrance and the sound of its rotors slowly faded in the distance. Jesse and Marty slowly stood up.

'I guess he made us after all,' Jesse said.

'This is great,' Marty groaned miserably. 'He's gonna have us for brunch...'

'I doubt that,' Jesse managed to joke. 'You know how sensitive his stomach is.'

'Go ahead, make jokes. Nothing like gallows humour before the execution...'

FOUR

Commander Altobelli filled his coffee mug with the pink magic of Pepto Bismol and sipped the concoction as he eyed the two men standing in front of his desk.

'Now let me get this straight,' he said, trying to keep calm. 'You were raising funds for the Police Charity Association . . .'

Marty and Jesse traded glances. They were having an equally difficult time keeping straight faces. 'Yes, sir,' they responded in unison.

Altobelli swilled down the last of his medication, then rose from his chair and wandered around his office, taking in the various scrolls, commendations, plaques, and trophies that attested to the twenty-nine and a half years of experience he had had with the police force. All in all, they were testimonies to the man's ability to know the facts and how to act on them. Still, he felt obligated to pose a rhetorical question to the two young officers fidgeting before him.

'Do I look like an idiot?' he demanded in a sudden outburst of anger.

'No, sir!' came the stereo response.

'Thank you.' Altobelli returned to his desk and plopped back into the cushioned embrace of his chair. He opened a side drawer and pulled out the bottle of Pepto Bismol, giving himself a refill. A calm settled back over him as he reflected, 'Walsh, Mach . . . believe it or not, I was a rookie once. I earned these stripes the hard way and I know all about street pressure. So don't misunderstand me . . . I can appreciate the need for you guys to blow off a little steam from time to time. We've all done it.'

'Yes, sir,' Mach said, relaxing slightly. Beside him, Marty

also let out a soft sigh of relief.

'But we didn't do it in department hours, dammit!' Altobelli launched back into the offensive. 'Maybe it's not practical for me to bust the entire division for this little display at the harbour . . . but I sure as hell plan to set an example. Guess how I'm going to do that?'

'Sir?' Marty said, taking a slight step forward. 'Perhaps if you let us explain . . .'

'Spare me, please.' Altobelli tossed the emptied bottle of antacid into his wastebasket, and with the same nonchalance told Mach and Walsh, 'You're both suspended for two weeks. Consider yourselves lucky that I'm going easy on you. Now, take a powder before I change my mind!'

The two officers turned and quietly padded out of the room, closing the door behind them. As they started down the hallway, Jesse clenched a fist and waved it at his partner.

'Well, nice play, Marty. Just what I wanted . . . a vacation without pay. A nice smudge on my record, thanks to your smooth-talking –'

'Hey, let up, okay?' Marty shot back. 'You didn't have to go through with it, you know. I didn't drug you. I didn't twist your arm.'

Jesse whacked the drinking fountain in the hallway with frustration. 'What a chump! I can't believe I did it!'

'Oh, come on,' Marty managed a laugh. 'Admit it, Jess. When you were making that jump, you were juiced to the max.'

As they bounded down the steps, Jesse recalled those compressed moments of concentrated intensity, and he had to grin at the memory. 'Yeah, it sure was one beaut of a jump, wasn't it?'

'That's the spirit!'

On their way out of the building, Marty stopped several times to collar officers who owed him money from their bets. Under the threat of exposure, he was able to get the men to pay up, albeit grudgingly.

'How much did we clear, anyway?' Jesse wanted to know as they left the station and headed for his old, renovated white Mustang.

'After I get all the bucks, it'll be nearly a paycheck apiece,' Marty calculated. 'And what's a little notoriety on the ol' record, anyway? In the long run, the big brass likes guys who show a little chutzpah now and then.'

'Whatever you say,' Jesse sighed. Marty got in the Mustang with him and they drove off. 'Now I just have to figure out what to do for the next two weeks.'

'I got an idea,' Marty suggested.

'What else is new?'

'Why not make the best of it?' Marty went on. 'I mean, let's get our dirt bikes outta the mothballs and haul 'em out to the desert for a good workout. We can eat up the sand until it gets boring, then cut out for some place further out in the sticks, rent some fishing gear and buy some beers . . . you know, live that life of Reilly . . .'

'Sounds decent,' Jesse admitted. He turned on to the freeway and picked up some speed. 'Of course, I don't think we should go so far into the boonies that we leave the ladies behind . . .'

'Don't worry, there's plenty of ladies out in the country,' Marty assured his partner. 'You'll have your hands full, I promise you.'

'Knowing you, Marty,' Jesse chuckled, 'that sounds more like a threat than a promise . . .'

FIVE

Although the Federal Institute of Law Enforcement Technological Development was a primary source of weapons research for every major governmental agency from the FBI and CIA to the Department of the Treasury, it was a low-profile organization that prided itself on its ability to stay out of the headlines. Its west coast regional offices bore out that fact quite clearly. Instead of setting up quarters in a highly-visible part of Los Angeles, FILE-TD, as the agency referred to itself, operated out of a modest suite located in a commercial centre lying between Rowland Heights and City of Industry in East LA. On one side of the building, their suitemates were two brothers who put out video games for adults, and on the other side was an agency that specialized in answering fan mail for soap opera stars.

Norman Tuttle arrived for work at precisely 8:59, as he had nearly every Monday and Tuesday morning for the past five years. On those days, he reported here rather than at his laboratory on the other side of town, usually to brief his superiors on his progress during the previous week and to receive any suggestions regarding revisions to his work or modifications he might be able to implement for weapons systems being developed by others within the agency. It was no small coincidence that Norman Tuttle's fictional hero was M, the supplier of those sundry, useful gadgets that invariably helped James Bond to bail out of whatever serious trouble his latest adventure might bring down on him. In fact, it was Tuttle's firm conviction that Jesse Mach was not even the palest of imitations of the great Mr Bond that filled him with such a sense of urgency as he flashed his security badge to the guard standing watch over the entrance to FILE-TD's inner sanctum.

'Is Mr Kirby in yet?' he asked out of habit, although he knew that the chances of his superior showing up at work on time were roughly equal to the prospects of taxes being lowered in the aftermath of a political campaign.

The guard, a Nordic-looking giant in a navy blue uniform, grinned as he let Norman through. 'Matter of fact, he is, Mr Tuttle.'

'What?' Norman gasped. 'You're joking, right?'

'Negative. He's in the conference room, waiting for you.' The guard looked around to make sure no one else was eavesdropping, then leaned to one side and whispered in Norman's ear, 'Man's in a real rush, if you know what I mean. I tried to tell him about the short we had in the alarm system last week and he damn near chewed my head off for interrupting his train of thought.'

'Oh, that's wonderful,' Norman groaned. 'Just what I need.'

'Just thought you'd want to know.'

'Thanks, Jimmy, I appreciate it.'

Norman continued down the corridor to the conference hall and let himself into the room. Elliot Kirby was seated at the head of the conference table, skimming over a legal pad opened up in front of him. There was a portable video monitor on the table next to him. When he saw Norman enter the room, he removed his bifocals and got right down to business.

'You got that footage of Mach, Tuttle?'

'Yes, sir, but –'

'Good, then let's cue it up and get the show on the road!' Kirby patted his palm on the viewer as if it were a pet in need of some attention. He was a lean, balding man dressed in an ash-grey pinstripe suit. He reminded Norman of Dwight Eisenhower with his feathers ruffled – someone unused to states of agitation and prone to over-reacting when the situation called for decisive action. Kirby was a consummate bureaucrat until the spectre of a deadline raised its ugly head, turning him into a holy terror. Norman realized at once that he wasn't going to have an easy time carrying out the scenario he'd concocted on the way to work. But he felt that he had to try.

'Well, our information about that harbour jump was correct,' Norman explained as he loaded his film into the viewing monitor. 'I got it all down, and I hope that after seeing Mach in action, you'll share my reservations...'

'Reservations?' Kirby barked. 'What the hell are you talking about, Tuttle? Reservations about what?'

The monitor was ready. Norman sat down and started up the film. 'Just watch, sir, and I'm sure you'll see for yourself.'

The footage flashing across the small screen was that of Jesse Mach riding out of the warehouse in his cape and painted helmet, taking a short lap around the four parked patrol cars and two ramps, then pausing a moment before making the actual jump. Norman was no slouch as a cameraman, and the tape faithfully captured the moment of infamy at the harbour prior to Commander Altobelli's untimely arrival.

'There it is, sir,' Norman said as he began rewinding the tape. He sounded like a prosecuting attorney presenting his closing arguments to a sceptical jury. 'I take it you can now understand why I think we should definitely consider another candidate for Operation Street Hawk. Jesse Mach just isn't the right material...'

'Nonsense, Tuttle!' Kirby protested, his face still twisted with the smile he'd gotten while watching Mach's jump. 'Hell, that was one fine piece of riding if you ask me...'

'Well, it's true that he *did* succeed at the jump, but that's hardly reason to overlook the other factors about the way he –'

'Tuttle, Tuttle,' Kirby scoffed as he began shuffling his legal pad and other assorted documents into his briefcase. 'Look, we've profiled hundreds of candidates and Jesse Mach shaped up as being the best man for the job. What you've shown me here only reinforces our position.'

Norman was crestfallen, but he tried not to show it. 'Just let me play this back for you in slow motion,' he offered, cueing up the video tape a second time. 'Watch closely and see how recklessly and irresponsibly he handles himself... to say nothing of the abusive way he tends to treat his equipment . . .'

Kirby chuckled as he stood up. 'Hell's bells, Norman, that's exactly what we're looking for! A cop with a test pilot mentality. A flyboy who's not afraid to push himself to the limit and beyond . . .'

The way Norman saw it, he had only one option left, and he went for it. 'But sir . . . I don't think I can work with a man like that.'

Kirby snapped his briefcase shut, then drummed his fingers briefly on the tooled leather. 'Tuttle, you're a damn good engineer . . .'

'The best, sir,' Norman agreed eagerly. 'That's why I was put *in charge* of this operation.'

Kirby ignored Tuttle's horn-tooting and went on, 'But you don't know a damn thing about the human factor. Listen to me, your boss. Jesse Mach has the right stuff. The Director wants him on this project, and so do I. Understood?'

Norman nodded bleakly, feeling his plan slipping away from him. He protested weakly, 'I was only thinking in terms of compatibility, sir. It is a crucial factor to consider, I think. And I have four years of my life invested in Street Hawk. It's my baby.'

'All the more reason for you to make sure we don't have to replace you with somebody who can carry out orders.' Kirby headed for the door. 'It was good seeing you, Norman. I have to catch the next flight back to Washington. I'm going to report that we have Jesse Mach lined up for the project. I'd hate to wind up with egg on my face for saying that. Know what I mean?'

Norman felt as if somebody had just tapped a hole in the base of his spine and drained everything out of him. He bobbed his head until Kirby had left the office, then sank slowly into the nearest seat, letting the grim realization wash over him like a polluted tide.

SIX

The closest off-road recreational area to Los Angeles was up north in desert country near Aqua Dulce. Not surprisingly, the sprawling facilities were jammed with people when Marty and Jesse arrived, hauling their bikes on a trailer hitched up to Marty's Jeep. Campers, Winnebagos, and pickups choked the asphalt parking lot, while off in the background, the desert was alive with the incessant whine of three-wheel all-terrain vehicles, dirt bikes, and dune buggies, which flitted across the sand like monstrous flies. Speakers from a hundred radios and tape players competed with the drone of labouring engines, bombarding the air with rock and roll, country, and some forms of music that defied description. To ward off the desert heat, liquids of various sorts flowed freely, adding to the carnival atmosphere. Sweat-soaked bikers swilled beers and sang along with their stereos when they weren't whistling at t-shirted mud-queens who preened like beauty contestants hustling votes. Cowboys in Stetsons and Frye boots sauntered to their off-road vehicles like rodeo champions getting ready to mount bucking broncos.

'Man, what a zoo!' Marty complained as he got out of his Jeep and helped Jesse unload their bikes. 'Let's not stick around here any longer than we have to.'

'I'm all for that.'

Both men were wearing padded motorcross gear and special riding boots. Once they had the bikes down on the asphalt and were giving the vehicles a quick once-over, Jesse and Marty found themselves surrounded by a small flock of teenage girls.

'Neat uniforms, guys,' one of the girls said, snapping

bubbles from a chaw of gum wedged between her ever-working jaws.

'Yeah,' another teenager gushed. 'Can we have a ride?'

Marty looked up from his work and shook his head. 'Sorry, ladies, but the last time we took passengers, they ended up falling off and wound up in hospital. Our insurance won't cover it.'

'Aw, come on. *Please*?'

'Sandy! Denise! Leave those men alone and get back over here!' a middle-aged woman called out from a Winnebago on the other side of the parking lot. The girls made faces behind their mother's back before shuffling away, taking their friends with them.

'Close call,' Marty laughed once he and Jesse were alone. 'We were a few seconds away from being attacked by adoring fans.'

'Yeah, right.' Jesse made a few final adjustments, then jumped on his kickstart and brought his Honda to life. 'I'm going to take a quick spin to get the bugs out. Maybe I'll stop by the shop and pick up a topo map so we can figure out where we want to split to.'

'Good idea. My Yamaha needs a little extra beating on, anyway.'

Jesse powered his dirt bike off the parking lot and out onto the nearest dunes. His carburettor was slightly out of adjustment, so he stopped several times to fine-tune it with a screwdriver from his kit. Once he had the cyle working to his satisfaction, he tackled a few of the hills, pushing the bike to its limits. Despite the congestion, which hampered his ability to sustain the kind of all-out riding he preferred, it was a welcome feeling to be back out on the dirt. If there was anything that rivalled the joys he felt as a motorcycle cop, it was the thrill of off-road riding. Marty had been right. This was just the sort of getaway he needed to take the sting out of their suspensions.

Once he'd finished his preliminary run, Jesse stopped off at the recreation area's shop, where he bought more gas for his bike along with a map detailing the topographical layout of the area and highlighting facilities located far from the maddening crowd. When he returned to the Jeep, he found Marty still tinkering with his Yamaha.

'I took it for a short spin, but it's still acting up a little,' Marty said with an edge of frustration in his voice. 'You think maybe you could give it a run and try to troubleshoot the problem for me?'

Jesse turned off his bike and handed Marty the topo map. 'Sure thing. Here, take a gander at this and plot our next move while I'm gone.'

'You got it.'

Marty unfolded the map as Jesse straddled the Yamaha and started it up. Once he'd ridden off, Marty quickly set aside the map and snickered to himself as he crept over to the Honda and began toying with the electrical system.

As Jesse ran the Yamaha through a few paces, he was being carefully watched by a familiar figure. Norman Tuttle was sitting behind the wheel of his car in the far corner of the parking lot, monitoring Jesse's ride through his binoculars.

'Look at him!' he anguished quietly to himself. 'How does he fix the engine? He kicks it! Oh, this is nice! He pops a wheelie in the middle of the parking lot! My God, what have I done wrong with my life to end up with him?'

Once Jesse had finished hotdogging, he ran the Yamaha through a few paces on the dunes, occasionally stopping to slap at the engine. Then he rode back to where Marty was sitting on the rear bumper of the Jeep, perusing the topo map.

'I don't know, Marty. It's running fine for me.' Jesse pointed to the engine. 'Only problem's a slight short on that black cable, but after I hit it a few times it quit acting up.'

'Hmm, well, thanks for checking it out anyway.'

Jesse climbed off the Yamaha and joined Marty in looking over the map. 'You figure out a good place to go?'

Marty nodded and pointed as he spoke. 'I like the sound of this Devil's Kitchen. Check out the hills there. Real squirrelly. Lots of gravel. Not many tourists, although it says here there's a fishing lodge next to this little lake.'

'Sounds good to me.' Jesse studied the map, committing the directions to memory. 'Let's go for it, okay?'

'Fine by me.' Marty mounted his Yamaha and kicked over

the engine. 'Twenty bucks says I beat you there.'

'You're on!'

Jesse climbed onto his Honda, but when he put his weight on the kickstart, the engine failed to start. He frowned with confusion and looked over at Marty, who was grinning diabolically.

'Oh yeah, I forgot to tell ya,' Marty said, 'I gave myself a little head start!'

As Marty raced off on his Yamaha, Jesse shook his head and let out a sigh of exasperation. 'What a guy...'

SEVEN

Far out in the middle of the desert was a rundown airstrip that had been abandoned by the military more than three decades before in favour of the facilities provided at nearby Edwards Air Force Base. Left to the elements, over the years the tarmac had buckled, victimized by the same blistering sun that had bleached the asphalt from its original pitch black to a faded grey. Weeds had pushed their way up through the cracks, attracting a makeshift ecosystem populated by insects, birds, lizards, and an occasional coyote or prairie dog to lord over the top of the food chain. Aside from the runway, there were also two vehicles that symbolized civilization's presence in the area. The rusted fuselage of an old fighter jet lay in a twisted heap off to one side of the landing strip, having been stripped long ago of any of its salvageable components.

The other vehicle was the gleaming black pickup truck that had been used in the robbery of the police van making its drug delivery the previous Sunday. Sitting behind the wheel of the truck was Anthony Corrido, who was casually dressed in jeans and a Pendleton shirt, over which he wore a bulky alpaca-trimmed jacket that effectively concealed the shoulder holster he was also wearing. He was a man with harsh features and an even harsher temperament. In crime circles, he was a fair-sized fish in a large-sized pond, who survived through a combination of reckless daring and a calculated intimidation of anyone below him who might entertain so much as the slightest notion of challenging him. He'd clawed his way to his current position of power, and he was prepared to keep clawing until he'd risen to the grand heights he envisioned as being part and parcel of his destiny.

His latest rendezvous with that destiny came in the form of a twin-engine Beechcraft that dipped out of the midday heavens seeking the least damaged stretch of the airfield on which to make a landing. Keeping a wary eye on the plane, Corrido started up his truck and drove through the tumbleweeds until he was within a dozen yards of where the aircraft had come to a halt. Remaining inside the pickup, Corrido reached for his gun and stared out through the tinted windows at the small portal in the side of the plane. Presently, the door opened and two men in business suits emerged, lowering a ladder and climbing down it to the runway. Once he was satisfied that he recognized the men, Corrido slipped the gun into its place of concealment, although he made sure the safety catch was released. If the need for gunplay were to arise, he wanted to be ready to come out firing.

'Afternoon, gents,' Corrido greeted the two men while the back shell of his truck opened and the bikers who had participated in the Sunday heist stepped out behind him. They were less discreet than their boss in displaying their firearms – .357 Magnums dangled threateningly in visible holsters beneath their armpits.

'Hello, Corrido,' the older of the businessmen said in greeting, shaking hands with the man in alpaca. 'I trust you have the stuff.'

'Could be,' Corrido said with a grin. 'There's one sure way to find out.'

The older businessman turned to his partner, who in turn reached inside his jacket. Within the space of half a second, three guns were suddenly aimed at him.

'I'm reaching for the cash,' he explained calmly. With slow caution, he pulled out a thick envelope and handed it to Corrido, who lowered his gun long enough to inspect the contents to his satisfaction.

'I'll take your word that it's all here,' he said.

'Good, and we'll take your word that we're buying the genuine article, not some stuff that's been pumped up with borax after somebody skimmed off a portion for themselves.'

Corrido snapped his fingers and his two associates went to the back of the pickup, pulling out the first of several white bricks of unadulterated cocaine. As the drug was being transferred from the truck to the plane, Corrido told the businessmen, 'Lucky for you, I can appreciate the need to talk tough. And as long as you're dishing it out, maybe you can take a little hard advice . . . If you think I make a nice ally, try crossing me sometime and find out what kind of an enemy I can turn out to be.'

'I don't think that will be necessary. Our boss has no qualms about dealing with you, and that's good enough for us. If we didn't ask you some tough questions, though, you'd think we were amateurs, and nothing could be further from the truth.'

When the last of the cocaine had been loaded aboard the Beechcraft, Corrido slipped the money envelope into his coat pocket and once again shook hands with the businessmen. He said, 'We'll have to go on meeting like this.'

'Then you can arrange for another delivery?'

Corrido nodded. 'Yeah, I think we're off to the start of a nice partnership. You just keep those greenbacks coming and I'll see that . . . damn, what's that?'

All five men turned and looked down the runway, hearing a high-pitched metallic whine drawing closer from behind a sandy knoll that bordered the east end of the old airfield. Suddenly Marty burst into view, riding over the crest on his speeding Yamaha. He didn't notice that he was being watched until he had made a slight leap that carried him from the top of the knoll down onto the tarmac. When he saw the plane and the truck, he skidded his bike to a quick stop.

'Get him!' Corrido commanded his men, who whipped out their Magnums and started firing rounds at Marty. Corrido hurried to his truck and slid in behind the wheel, cursing under his breath as he started up the engine. 'Damn fool sure as hell picked the wrong time and place to go joy-riding . . .'

Marty had been a cop long enough to put two and two together and realize what he'd blundered upon, and as the first bullets pocked the asphalt around him, he cranked his throttle wide-open and rode off as quickly as physically possible. Behind him, he could hear the pickup roaring into the chase.

'Wherever you are, Jesse,' he muttered under his breath, 'I hope to hell you got your bike fixed faster than I planned for you to . . .'

EIGHT

Marty had done a good job of putting the Honda out of commission. As he struggled to rework the wiring and get the bike started, Jesse's mind raced with scenarios for the sort of revenge he was going to wreak on his friend once he caught up with him. Engrossed as he was, Jesse didn't notice that he was being wached until Norman Tuttle moved in close enough to throw a shadow aross the Honda.

'Hey, do you mind?' Jesse said as he sorted through his toolbox for a ratchet wrench. 'You're blocking my light.'

'Sorry,' Norman apologized, moving to one side. When he saw Jesse take one of the wrenches and turn back to the cycle, he added, 'That one's too small. You'll need a seven-sixteenths to get at the electrical box.'

Jesse glanced up at his visitor, holding one hand over his eyebrows to screen out the slanting rays of the midday sun. 'Thanks for the tip, pal, but I know my bike.'

'Just trying to be helpful.'

'Right.' Jesse applied the wrench to the nut holding a metal plate over the electrical fusebox. His ears flushed red as he realized the wrench was indeed the wrong size.

'Like I said,' Norman told him. 'A seven-sixteenths.'

Jesse went back to his toolbox and began rummaging for the right wrench. When Norman continued to loom over him, he cracked, 'Don't you have a picnic or something to go to?'

Norman squatted onto his haunches. 'Actually, I'm here to see you.'

'Oh, is that a fact?' Jesse freed the nut from the electrical plate and began inspecting the fuses. 'Let me guess, you represent my long-lost uncle and you have a cheque for a million dollars he willed to me before he died, right?'

Norman swallowed hard, fighting back an overwhelming desire to walk off and take his chances with telling Kirby that Jesse wasn't available for Project Street Hawk. He won the fight and held his ground, forging ahead. 'My name is Norman Tuttle. I'm a research engineer, employed by the Federal Institute of Law Enforcement Technological Development. Here, let me show you my identification...'

'Better yet, Norman, why don't you hand me that hammer?'

'You don't seem to understand.' Norman flashed a laminated nametag with his picture and the FILE-TD logo next to it. 'I'm here on official business.'

'That's really great,' Jesse drawled sarcastically. 'Look, if you want to bend my ear, fine, but you're gonna have to help me while you're at it, okay?'

Norman sighed. After he put away his i.d., he glanced over the assortment of grimy tools cluttering the toolbox. For someone who routinely polished his working gear and kept it meticulously stored, the sight was more than slightly disconcerting. 'Which hammer?' he asked, making little effort to conceal his displeasure. 'The greasy ballpeen or the chewed-up rubber mallet?'

Jesse ignored the jibe and held his hand out, 'The heavy one.'

Norman picked up the rubber mallet as if it were a dead rat and handed it to Jesse, who promptly used it to bang away at the electrical housing.

'Are you always this abusive to your equipment?' Norman asked.

'Only when it doesn't work, Norman.' Once he had readjusted the housing to his satisfation, Jesse set down the hammer and went back to work with the ratchet.

'I'm the project co-ordinator of a top-secret development programme that's right up your alley,' Norman explained. 'The Director's given me total control over the entire operation... proposal, design, execution – everything. Well, almost everything. *You* were hand-picked by a selection committee that reviewed more than three hundred and fifty other candidates.'

Jesse nodded sceptically. 'Hey, I get junk mail every other day from people trying to tell me I'm uniquely qualified to be a sucker for their sales pitch. You want to flatter me, you're gonna have to come up with something better than that.' He finished inspecting all the fuses and electrical connections, correcting the problems Marty had created, then slapped the metal plate back in place and tightened it.

'I even picked the code name,' Norman lobbied, talking through gritted teeth. 'Street Hawk . . . like the bird of prey.'

'Sounds real cute, Norman.' Jesse put on his helmet and mounted the Honda. 'Kinda reminds me of something out of my old Marvel comics.'

'Well, this is far from comic book frivolities, I can assure you. I'm talking about a top-priority clandestine operation. You'd be working independent of local authorities. Just me and you.'

'A regular Batman and Robin, eh?' Jesse snickered as he kicked over his engine, starting it on the first try. 'Thanks for the offer Norm, buddy, but I'm not interested.'

'Not interested? But I haven't even told you about the operation yet!' Norman protested.

'I've heard enough,' Jesse replied over the sound of his bike. 'Sorry, but I don't trust Feds. You never know whose side they're on. Listen, could you do me a favour and toss those tools back in the box and put 'em in the back of that Jeep over by the Airstream? I'm running a little behind schedule.'

'But . . .'

'Thanks, Norman.' With a wave of his hand, Jesse rode off weaving through the crowd and out onto the sand, where he headed off in the same direction Marty had taken some time before. Norman watched him, relief matching his frustration.

'I tried, Mr Kirby,' he murmured to himself. 'You can't say I didn't try . . .'

The Honda was running fine now, and Jesse powered it past the other riders ravaging the desert around the recreation centre. Recalling the layout of the topo map, he struck a course that ran adjacent to a series of steel-girded electrical towers carrying high-power lines across the desert. As he followed the extra-terrestrial-looking towers, Jesse wondered about his brief encounter with Norman Tuttle. It didn't seem to make any sense to him. Why would a government intelligence agency be interested in him, especially to the extent Tuttle claimed they were? Granted, he was a cop, but so were a few million other Americans. Other than that, he didn't see himself as having any outstanding qualities, unless one considered a few biking trophies he'd won over the years. And how had this Tuttle fellow tracked him down to the recreation area in the first place? The more he thought about it, the more Jesse became convinced that Marty had put Tuttle up to the charade as another way of delaying him from taking off. Marty would go to any lengths to win a bet.

Spotting a tell-tale knoll off to his right, Jesse veered away from the electrical conductors. He soon came across the treadmarks left by Marty earlier, and as he followed them, he was suddenly distracted by the abrupt appearance of a Beechcraft airplane from the other side of the knoll. It was just taking off, and it flew low across the desert, then changed its course and began to bear down on Jesse.

'Hey, what gives?' Jesse shouted, turning quickly and opening up the throttle to race away from the plane. It swooped down low, missing him by a good twenty yards, then banked away and streaked toward the ragged trail of clouds stretching across the afternoon sky. Jesse watched until the plane shrank to a speck, then rode back to where he could pick up Marty's trail. He cleared the knoll and rode across the deserted airstrip. When he saw the twin treadmarks of a second vehicle heading in the same direction Marty had travelled, Jesse felt an instinctive jolt of paranoia shoot along the length of his spine. Both sets of tracks strayed off the other side of the airstrip and headed toward a gorge that cut through the desert floor like a ripped seam of earth. To his horror, he soon discovered that while both vehicles had travelled to the edge of a precipice overlooking the gorge, only the truck's tracks led away from the cliff. Jesse rode to the lip of the precipice and glanced downward.

More than twenty yards down the steep pitch of the embankment, Marty lay in a grotesquely twisted position next to his crumpled Yamaha. Neither Marty nor the bike were moving.

'Marty . . .'

Stunned by the impact of what he had just seen, Jesse was slow to realize that the black pickup responsible for Marty's demise had roared out from behind a cluster of boulders and was heading directly for him. By the time he heard the truck over the growl of his own engine, it was too late for Jesse to avoid the same fate that had befallen his friend. He had only time enough to whirl about and catch a brief glimpse of the dark blur charging toward him, before there was a splintering crash and he felt himself being flung into a black, noiseless void.

NINE

Fragments of sensation, shreds of barely-grasped memories flitted through Jesse's mind as he drifted in and out of consciousness . . .

The buzz of rotors from an approaching helicopter, followed by the sting of sand sent flying by the blades' downwash . . .

Footsteps crunching the gravel around him; a man's voice off in the distance. 'This one's dead . . .'

'I think we have a pulse over here.' The vague sense of pressure against his wrist. 'His leg's a mess, though. Musta had the bike land on it . . .'

Many voices whispering above him, their words lost in a jumble . . .

A feeling of weightlessness, then the tug of straps binding him to a stretcher . . .

'If we can get him under the knife in time, I think there's a chance . . .'

Weightless again, swaying to and fro, the chopper droning above him, dangling him by a cord as it floats above the desert.

A chill in the air; wind against his face . . .

Half-opened eyes and a glimpse of vibrant colours, wondering, 'Am I dead?' Realizing it's the setting sun . . .

Dreams of reckless biking, sharing laughter with Marty, casting fish lures out into a tranquil lake . . .

An explosion of new sounds, filled with the echo of enclosed walls; a hospital corridor . . .

'Blood pressure down. Pulse irregular . . .'

Rolling on a gurney, eyes looking up at the ceiling, where fluorescent lights float by like clouds; something pressed against his mouth and the base of his nose, making it easy to breathe...

A huddle of men in white with surgical masks, conferring over his legs. 'We'll do what we can, but we have to be prepared to amputate...'

Trying to shout, but nothing comes out. Another mask and the hiss of gas, bringing new darkness so complete that even dreams can't intrude...

'Congratulations, doc. Great work!'

'He might be able to walk with a limp and a cane, but he'll never ride again...'

And then he awoke, fully conscious for the first time in more than twenty-four hours. He was in a recovery room, his left leg swathed in layers of gauze and surgical tape. He was alone. The room was stark white, with a single bouquet of flowers on the nightstand by his bed. The television was on with the volume turned down low, cartoons flashing across its screen. He sat still a long while, piecing things together. Once he'd figured out what had happened, he signalled for a nurse to come and confirm his suspicions. Yes, he had required surgery on his knee. Yes, the surgery had been successful, to a degree. Yes, it was likely that the damage was so severe that he couldn't hope for a full recovery. And, yes, Marty was dead.

'Damn.' Jesse asked to be left alone and turned off the television. In the silence, he wept at the loss of his closest friend and felt a growing anger at the circumstances of Marty's death. Why? Why did it have to happen? Dammit, it wasn't fair!

His doctor stopped by later to describe the nature of his injuries, but Jesse couldn't sort through all the technical jargon and asked for the bottom line, in layman's terms.

'You've got a bum knee,' the doctor told him. 'As bum as they come. But I don't have to remind you just how lucky you were to have only that and a mild concussion.'

'Yeah, I could be dead, right?' Jesse glared at the doctor. 'Why'd I get off so easy when Marty was killed?'

'There were as many differences between your crashes as there were similarities,' the doctor confided. 'Most importantly, whatever knocked you off the cliff only gave your bike a glancing blow. Your friend, I'm afraid, was hit broadside. He was killed instantly . . . probably didn't feel a thing, not that that's much of a consolation.'

Jesse clenched his hand into a fist and slammed it into the pillow at his side. 'Did they catch them?' he asked angrily. 'The guys who did this?'

The doctor shook his head. 'I'm afraid not. It was well over an hour after you were hit that someone spotted you and your friend . . .'

Filled with a sense of determination, Jesse started to climb out of bed, grimacing at the pain in his leg. 'Where're my clothes?'

'Easy, there,' the doctor said. 'You've just been through the wringer, my friend. You aren't going to just get up and walk out of here.'

'What do you mean?'

'I mean that you're going to have to stay here at least for the rest of the week. You've lost a lot of blood and had a few other minor injuries as well. It'd be best if you rested up and let us keep you under observation. In a couple of days we'll try out some physiotherapy and set you up with a rehabilitation programme. With a little patience, you'll have most of your strength back in no time.'

Jesse slumped back onto the bed and stared forlornly at the wrapping around his knee. 'It won't be soon enough . . .'

TEN

'You want me to get the door?'

Jesse looked over at Officer Mike Holt, a longtime colleague. They were in Holt's patrol car. He'd picked up Jesse at the hospital and taken him to the police station.

'Thanks, Mike,' Jesse said, opening the door on his own. 'I can manage.'

'Good to see you up and around again, Jess.'

With minor difficulty, Jesse climbed out of the car and steadied himself on the sidewalk, relying on a cane for balance. He was wearing a suit Mike had brought to the hospital for him, but even through the herringbone it was easy to see that his left leg was wrapped so securely he couldn't bend it.

'Go get 'em, Mike!' Jesse closed the door and waved to Holt as the officer drove off.

Returning to the station for the first time since his suspension was a bittersweet experience. It was good to see the concern in old, familiar faces and to hear the well-wishing that greeted him wherever he went, but his limp was a source of frustration and without the boisterous presence of Marty, the station seemed somehow colder, more forbidding. Farnsworth filled him in on the details concerning Marty's funeral – buried with honours; motorcycle parade flanking the hearse on the way to the cemetery; a few of the good old times recalled at the grave before the coffin had been lowered; not a dry eye in the house by the time all was said and done.

'Not gonna be the same without that crazy nut around tryin' to bilk me outta my paycheck,' Farnsworth concluded, forcing a chuckle. 'Hell, I'll bet he'll have angels bettin' their haloes on whether or not we're gonna join him when we kick... either that or he'll be tryin' the same scam with the devil's pitchforks, eh?'

'Yeah, probably,' Jesse said as he pushed a button for the elevator.

'Well, I gotta split. You meetin' with the chief?'

Jesse nodded.

'Good luck, Mach. I mean it.'

'Thanks.'

Altobelli was out of his office when Jesse stopped by, but he was expected back shortly and Jesse was asked to wait for him. Left alone in the office, Jesse wandered to the window and stared out at the driveway that banked up from the station's underground garage. A pair of motorcycle cops guided their Kawasakis up the incline, then disappeared down the street. Jesse looked away, biting his lower lip.

'Sorry, Mach,' the commander called out as he strode into the room, cranking the top off a fresh bottle of Pepto Bismol. 'I got held up.'

'They get away with much?'

'Huh?' Altobelli splashed some of the pink ooze into his coffee mug, then caught the joke. 'Oh, right. Held up. Glad to see you didn't lose your sense of humour, Mach. You look good, I have to say.'

'Thanks.' Jesse waited until the commander had sat down and had his first sip, then asked the question foremost on his mind. 'How's the investigation going?'

Altobelli shrugged. 'I.A.'s got it.'

'Internal Affairs?' Jesse gasped. 'What's it doing there?'

'Now don't get excited! It's purely routine.' Altobelli wiped a fleck of pink from his upper lip. 'They want to make sure you guys weren't involved in anything.'

'What!'

'Don't bite my head off about it! You're the ones who had the bright idea of staging that First Annual Harbour Jump and taking bets on it. And everybody knows Marty was always looking for a good wager. I.A. just needs to make sure that what happened out there in the desert wasn't related to anything that's gonna reflect bad on the department.'

Jesse snorted contemptuously. 'Oh, that's rich! Marty gets buried with honours and you put on a great show of compassion so you can milk some public relations out of it, and on the side you're accusing him and me of doing dirt!'

'Nobody's accusing anybody of anything,' Altobelli maintained.

'Oh, man, this stinks!'

'I know you guys were clean, but this has to be done by the book, and let's face it, the timing couldn't have been worse, what with the two of you on suspension at the time.'

Jesse started pacing, leaning heavily on the cane with each step to favour his bad leg. 'I.A. isn't going to get to the bottom of this, and we both know it! My best friend's dead and finding his killer's going to get a lower priority than running speed traps!'

'I'll do what I can, Mach.'

Jesse stopped pacing and leaned across his commander's desk. 'I want to get back to work.'

'I figured as much when you called.' Altobelli leaned back in his chair and picked up a manila folder off his desk. 'I can lift your suspension, but you're not gonna like your assignment, I can promise you.'

'Where'd you stick me?'

Altobelli opened the file, but he already knew the information contained in it. 'Public Relations. Same rank and salary.'

Jesse lowered himself into the chair behind him and shook his head. He'd been expecting this, but now that it was official, the news still came as a crushing blow. 'What am I going to do in Public Relations?' he moaned. 'I'm a motorcycle cop. All I know is the street! You can't stick me with those pencil pushers down on the ground floor!'

'It's done, Mach.' Altobelli was sounding forceful, but in a compassionate sort of way. Referring to the top sheet in the file, he went on, 'I saw your medical record, Jesse. Your knee's a mess. It's been totalled, and there's no way you can operate a bike in that condition. I can't put you back on the street.'

'If I can't ride a bike, I can still ride patrol in a cruiser. Team me up with Mike Holt...'

'Can't do it, Jesse. Face it, that knee's put you out of the field.' Altobelli stared hard at Jesse. 'I don't like being the carrier of bad news, especially to a decent kid like you with the makings of a good cop. But you have to face facts. You can take the new job, or you can go home. It's your choice...'

ELEVEN

Jesse reported to work at the station's Public Relations office the following morning. Instead of his blue uniform, he wore the same suit he'd worn the day before. It was the only suit he owned, for that matter, and when Farnsworth presented him with some of the belated payments from the harbour jump, Jesse figured that the majority was going to have to go towards expanding his wardrobe. The thought depressed him, and when he linked up with Sandy McCoy for an initiation and the intricacies of his new position, it was all he could do to feign interest. She was quick to pick up on his feelings, and as they started down the hallway to what would be his office, she sympathized, 'Sorry that things had to turn out this way for you, Jesse. I know your heart's still set on being a motorcycle cop...'

'Yeah, too bad my knee's not set on it, too, huh?' Jesse had seen Sandy around the station frequently over the past few years, and there had been times when he had even been intrigued enough by her to entertain notions of asking her out. He'd never followed through on such notions, though, and now that they were working together, his resentment over his assignment made it difficult to still find her attractive.

Sandy let Jesse's remark slip by without a response. As they continued down the corridor, she launched into a spiel about public relations work. 'We deal mainly with the media,' she explained. 'Newspapers, radio, and television. But we also like to get out into the community as much as possible... speaking at Neighbourhood Watch gatherings; setting up department tours; organizing fundraisers and charity events like the Police Celebrity Golf Tournament we're putting on next weekend... Am I going too fast for you?'

'No, I'm only partially crippled,' Jesse snapped, dragging his stiff leg along as he put his weight against his walking cane. He'd got used to the stick and was able to move with certainty despite his pronounced limp.

'I'm sorry,' Sandy apologized. 'I didn't mean it that way.'

'I know what you meant...'

Sandy stopped and stepped in front of Jesse, blocking his way. 'Look,' she said sternly. 'I didn't ask for this.'

'And neither did I!'

'Okay, fine...' They suspended their argument temporarily as a pair of meter maids walked by, then Sandy resumed, 'But since we're stuck with each other, why don't we at least try to make the best of it?'

Before Jesse had a chance to respond, a middle-aged man in a three-piece suit ambled toward them, grinning widely at Sandy. 'Well, hello, Ms McCoy...'

Sandy nodded a greeting back. 'Commissioner Miller. Good to see you. I was just briefing Officer Mach on his new responsibilities...'

'Of course.' Miller's smile faded slightly as he turned to Jesse. 'Good to have you back on the force, Mach. Sorry about your partner.'

'Thanks,' Jesse mumbled. He had never cared much for the commissioner, who always struck him as being vain and conservative to a fault... not necessarily in that order.

'It's a whole new ball game on the inside, Mach,' Miller advised. 'But I have a gut feeling you're going to fit right in.'

'Yes, sir. I'm really looking forward to the Police Celebrity Golf Tournament this year,' Jesse warbled with mock enthusiasm. 'I'm even thinking of buying a set of clubs.'

Sandy flinched at the sarcasm, but Commissioner Miller didn't seem to notice. 'Good, glad to hear it, Mach! Well, I have to run.' He draped his arm briefly on Jesse's shoulder. 'Listen, if I can be of any help at all, you know where my office is.'

Jesse nodded.

'Commissioner,' Sandy reminded Miller, 'don't forget our lunch meeting Tuesday. We really need to talk about that

City Council presentation.'

'Right. I'm sure my secretary has it on my schedule.'

Once Miller was out of earshot, Sandy turned to Jesse and said, 'Well, it's a comfort to know that you're being obnoxious with everyone and not just me.'

'Look, I'm sorry,' Jesse told her. 'This all needs some getting used to, that's all. I'm not always like this, you know.'

'That's a relief. Now, where were we?'

'Making the best of it,' Jesse prompted. 'And I agree. We might as well do that...'

'Good.' They continued down to the end of the hallway, where Sandy opened the door to a small, cramped room filled with filing cabinets, a small desk, and a telephone. The one wall that wasn't blocked by furniture was covered with a cork bulletin board filled with flyers, notes, telephone numbers, business cards, and other clutter. 'This is your base of operations. It's a little cosy, but you'll be so busy you'll hardly have time to notice.'

Jesse took in the cubicle with a wary eye, then sat down in the wooden swivel chair in front of the desk. 'Well, there's no window, so I won't have to worry about seeing what I'm missing...'

TWELVE

Jesse was so wound up by the end of the day that he couldn't help but take up an offer by Farnsworth and Mike Holt to join a few officers for a round or two of off-duty drinks at their favourite watering hole, The Come-on Inn. It was a small, seedy establishment with dim lights, a range of British ales on tap, three dog-eared dartboards, and the best jukebox in all of Los Angeles. Jesse often came here after work, usually with Marty, who had the habit of feeding the jukebox a handful of quarters and punching out every Motown song dating back to his early youth in Detroit. In Marty's memory, tonight Farnsworth cued up those same songs and led the first of several toasts to their departed comrade. Jesse felt strange in the midst of the testimonials, and for the most part sat silently, sipping his Watney beer between bites of the shepherd's pie he'd ordered for supper. His discomfort progressed to a state of severe depression as the conversation around him inevitably drifted to gossip about the latest happenings out on the street. The more those around him loosened up and joked with one another, the more Jesse withdrew into himself. Finally he couldn't take it any more. He excused himself, claiming he wasn't feeling well because he had mixed alcohol with the pain-killers he was supposedly taking for his knee.

Farnsworth followed Jesse out of the bar and caught up with him near Mach's Mustang.

'Hey, Jess? You sure you're okay? Maybe I should drive you.'

'I don't need anybody's help, dammit!' Jesse exploded, pounding his fist on the hood.

Farnsworth backpedalled away from Jesse, throwing his hands up at his sides as if he were under arrest. 'Okay, okay. I was just tryin' to be a friend, Jesse, that's all . . .'

Jesse sighed as he opened his door. 'I know, Farny. I'm sorry. I guess I still need some more time to get used to the way everything's changed.'

'That's cool. Hell, it can't have been easy, goin' through everything that's come down on you.' Farnsworth grinned and punched Jesse lightly on the shoulder. 'Tough it out. I'm sure you'll pull through in flyin' colours.'

'I appreciate the vote of confidence.' Jesse slid in behind the wheel of his Mustang and started the engine. Rolling down his window, he told Farnsworth, 'Now get back in there with the others. Here's a quarter. Put on some Four Tops for Marty, okay?'

'Sure thing, Mach.'

On his way home, Jesse stopped off at the market to pick up some groceries. It was next to impossible for him to use the cane while pushing a grocery cart, and he ended up putting the cane in the cart and relying on the cart for support. It worked for the most part, but as he was rounding the corner near the produce section, the cart's front wheels momentarily jammed and Jesse almost knocked over a display case of boxed raisins trying to maintain his balance. A child riding in a cart just down the aisle started laughing at him until her mother scolded her into silence. Jesse righted the wheels on his cart and hurried through the check-out line. He'd only bought a sackful of groceries, most of it fruit, so he was able to walk out holding the bag in one arm while using the cane with the other. By now it was dark, and as he stepped down from the kerb leading to the parking lot, Jesse heard the bleat of sirens and looked out at the street, where a pair of motorcycle cops glided majestically by, answering a call from the station dispatcher. Jesse stared at the officers with longing and envy, wishing there was some way he could be out there.

The screeching of brakes and the blare of an angry horn wrenched Jesse from his reverie. A car had nearly collided with him. As he spun about to get out of the way, Jesse lost his grip on his groceries. The bag tumbled from his grasp and landed on the pavement, sending grapefruit and oranges rolling off in all directions.

'What's your problem, man!' the driver roared out his window at Jesse. 'Why don't you watch where you're going?'

Jesse just stared at the other man as he drove off. Flushed with a sudden rage, he kicked at his fallen produce and left it on the ground, then stormed off to his Mustang. He swore a blue streak all the way back to his apartment complex, venting the day's anger. As he pulled into the underground garage and parked, he felt mildly purged. But when he stepped out of his Mustang and saw someone walk out of the shadows towards him, the bile rose in his throat.

'Good evening, Mr Mach... remember me? Norman Tuttle... the Fed. Can we talk?'

Jesse talked with his fist, sending Norman spinning to the ground with a fierce right cross. As Tuttle slowly sat up and rubbed his chin, Jesse loomed over him, hands clenched into fists. 'You picked the wrong time, pal, that's all I have to say!'

Norman's lower lip was bleeding, and he took out a handkerchief to staunch the flow of blood. His phone call to Elliot Kirby in Washington the other night had left him with the unmistakable impression that if he didn't secure Jesse Mach for Operation Street Hawk, the project stood a good chance of being taken out of his hands. With stakes that high, Norman was willing to suffer the indignities of being knocked down and scorned... barely.

'Well, Mr Mach, now that you've had your say, do you think maybe I could have mine...?'

THIRTEEN

Norman stood before the fireplace mantel in Jesse's apartment, looking over the array of trophies and plaques displayed there. Most of the figurines on the trophies were miniature motorcycle riders, frozen in motion astride dirt bikes of various sizes.

'Quite a collection you have here, Jesse.'

Jesse entered the living room from the kitchen, carrying two beers. He handed one to Norman. 'Here, after that punch it's the least I can do for you. That lip okay?'

Norman pressed the cold can against his mouth, numbing the throb in his lower lip, which had stopped bleeding but had swollen to almost twice its normal size. 'I'll live. Are you sure you didn't box on the side while you were winning all these trophies?'

'I just caught you when you weren't looking. My apologies again.'

'Forget it.' Norman popped his can open, then held it out for a toast. 'Cheers.'

'Cheers.' They clanked cans, then Norman looked back at the trophies as he took his first sip of beer.

'Which one of these trophies is the first one you ever won?'

Jesse went over to the mantel and picked up a small statuette of a bronzed rider holding a motorcross helmet under his arm as he stood proud and tall on a small wooden pedestal. 'Got this when I was fourteen. Worked my way up to the Internationals by the time I was eighteen. That's where I got this sucker...'

Norman looked at the wall plaque Jesse had pointed to. It showed a rider in full relief. The etched lettering below the figure proclaimed that Jesse Mach had won the award for Best Overall Performer. 'Very impressive, Jesse.'

'Not really,' Jesse said. 'Considering some of the things I did to win that trophy, I should have had my head examined. Besides, motorcross is a real flash-in-the-pan sort of pastime. Most riders burn out by the time they're twenty-two...'

'Is that why you stopped competing?'

'No, I really gave it up because I wanted to be a cop.' Jesse took a long drink, then settled down into a well-worn leather chair. 'But, let's face it, Norman... you didn't come here to gawk at my trophies. What's on your mind?'

Norman sat on the edge of the couch across from Jesse, leaning forward with his hands clasped across his knees. 'Jesse, do you remember what we were talking about back at the recreation area? Operation Street Hawk?'

'Yeah, I remember... vaguely.'

'Well, the offer still stands.'

Jesse smirked as he reached for his cane and gently tapped his injured leg. 'Haven't you noticed? No knee. I'm not sure what your project is all about, but unless it has something to do with pushing a pencil, I won't be of much help. For that matter, I think you'd find out real quick that paperwork isn't my strong suit, anyway.'

'I know all about your knee, Jesse. I've seen the medical reports.'

'You what?'

'I told you I was involved with Intelligence,' Norman reminded Jesse. 'When we need vital data, we have a way of getting our hands on it.'

'You don't know how relieved that makes me feel,' Jesse drawled cynically. 'Okay, I'll bite. If you know I've got a bum knee, what are you doing here?'

Norman finished his beer and set the can down, then told Jesse, 'There's a new prosthesis that can give you a full range of motion in your left leg.'

'Right.' Jesse rolled his eyes. 'I'll bet it was developed by a screenwriter from an old episode of *The Six Million Dollar Man*, eh?'

Norman went to the attaché case he'd brought with him

and pulled out a thick pamphlet from one of the side pockets. Handing the document to Jesse, he said, 'It's all explained here, and it's totally legitimate. Naturally, we'd be willing to foot the bill for the surgery, provided you'd be willing, in turn, to commit yourself to Operation Street Hawk.'

'A little bit of bribery, is that it?' Jesse skimmed through the folder, noting the detailed diagrams of not only the prosthesis, but also the surgical procedure by which it would be implanted. 'How come my doctors didn't bother to mention this to me?'

'Because it's an experimental project at the moment.'

'Of course . . . and I'm supposed to be the first guinea pig.' Jesse folded up the pamphlet and handed it back to Norman. 'No thanks.'

'To date, the prosthesis has been used on twenty-five test subjects, and in all but one instance the results were as good or better than expectations. In the one other case, the patient was still as well off as he was prior to surgery. FDA approval will probably be forthcoming in the next two years.'

'Why should I believe you?' Jesse wondered aloud. 'Why are you going to all this trouble on my account anyway? I don't get it.'

'I tried to explain this to you before,' Norman said. 'Certain people in our organization are convinced, by virtue of their intensive personnel search, that you have what our project needs. The phrase they like to use is that you have the so-called "right stuff".'

'Go ahead, flattery will get you everywhere.' Jesse finished his beer, then crushed the can and tossed it across the room, where it bounced off the wall and landed neatly in a wastebasket. 'So, tell me, Norman . . . what would I be doing once I went through this little Frankenstein ordeal with your mad doctors?'

'You'd be testing a highly sophisticated piece of equipment,' Norman said. 'If you're interested, I can show it to you.'

Jesse shrugged his shoulders and got up from his chair. 'Well, there're only re-runs on the tube tonight . . . let's do it . . .'

FOURTEEN

Ironically, when Norman Tuttle took Jesse to the location where he based his Street Hawk operations, they were less than three blocks away from where the cocaine heist had taken place the week before. Norman pulled his station wagon to a stop near the back loading dock of an old, dilapidated warehouse that looked nearly a generation past its prime. As he got out of the station wagon and looked around, Jesse whistled slowly.

'This hardly looks like the kind of place in which one's likely to come across a highly sophisticated piece of equipment, Norman.'

'That's the idea,' Norman said, sorting through his keys as he led Jesse to a small side door, dimly lit by a naked bulb that was under constant bombardment by a squadron of moths and June bugs. He opened the door and gestured for Jesse to enter, telling him, 'Welcome to Command Centre.'

After walking down an unadorned, drab hallway, Jesse stepped through a doorway into a large, darkened enclosure. Behind him, Norman moved over to a control box and threw several marked power switches. The building hummed with the buzz of electricity surging through a pair of high-power generators feeding off the main current. Banks of fluorescent lights flickered on, bathing the main room in a warm, thorough glow.

'Man, I don't believe this!' Jesse's eyes widened as he took in the rows of computers, mounted scanning monitors, and other pieces of high-tech equipment glinting in the lights. Console lights glowed like dozens of small eyes, and the various machines gave off competing drones and hums as an electrical current ran through them.

'It's all quite real, I assure you,' Norman said, visibly pleased with Jesse's awe.

'And what's this over here?' Jesse said as he approached the main focal point of the room, a massive control module consisting of computer banks, viewing screens, closed-circuit camera equipment, and enough other technological paraphernalia to make an electronics wizard drool. 'Looks like the bridge of the Star Ship Enterprise.'

'This is my Mount Olympus,' Norman boasted solemnly as he activated a rheostat switch, lighting up a huge vector map on the main viewing screen. 'From here, I can monitor activity throughout the entire city by merely adjusting my controls.'

'That's pretty wild business, Norman.' Jesse sat down in the padded chair overlooking the module. 'You didn't strike me as the Roman deity type.'

'Mount Olympus was home of the Greek gods, not the Roman,' Norman corrected. 'And please, don't touch anything. You're looking at close to three million dollars' worth of equipment.'

'I believe it,' Jesse said. 'This sure is some Erector set. Say, what's that blinking red light up in the corner on that map there?'

Norman leaned over the control board and arranged for a section of the map to be magnified on the screen several times until it was clear that the blinking light was situated at a spot on the map representing the warehouse in which they were now standing. 'That light, Jesse, is what monitors the location of Street Hawk. Perhaps it's time you had a look at it.'

'Amen to that.'

Norman punched up another command on the module, and soon both men were alerted by a grating sound behind them. They turned to see an eerie cloud of smoke spilling from inside a cavity behind the far wall. The wall itself was swivelling about, allowing an even brighter light to flood the main room. Jesse gaped in wonder as the smoke began to clear, revealing a revolving platform upon which rested a sleek black motorcycle of the sort he had never laid eyes upon before. In his time, Jesse had seen perhaps five hundred different makes of motorcycle, but this one was unlike any of the others. Sleek in design, it nonetheless carried a number of built-in compartments containing systems that Jesse could only guess at. As more and more of the smoke fell away from it and the platform ceased its revolving, Jesse strode forward for a closer look.

'My God, Norman, where did you come across this beauty? Man, what a motorcycle!'

'I made it,' Norman replied succinctly. 'And you'll find that it's far more than just a motorcycle. Specifically it's an all-terrain pursuit vehicle.'

'A rose by any other name...' Despite Norman's earlier warning, Jesse couldn't help but touch the bike. He ran a finger gently along the aerodynamic curves. 'Look, Norman, call it what you want. I want to ride it.'

'I thought you might,' Norman grinned, feeling for the first time since he'd met the younger man that he now held the upper hand. 'Of course, you realize there's a price to be paid for that privilege.'

'You want me to be a test rider,' Jesse guessed. 'A flyboy on two wheels...'

'My superior has used a similar term, so I would have to say that's an accurate assessment, yes.' Norman pulled a single sheet of paper from his attaché case and held it before Jesse. 'This is a standard government contract. You should read it over carefully, then sign it. It basically says that you've agreed to become a test rider for FILE-TD and that you are willing to accept the responsibility for any and all dangers that come with the assignment.'

'Don't start drowning me in small print, Norman. When can I ride the bike?'

'As I said, Jesse, there are certain pre-conditions before I can even let you sit on Street Hawk...'

'Street Hawk... Street Hawk.' Jesse circled the bike, letting its name roll about on the end of his tongue. 'Yeah, I can see it. Nice name. Now when can I ride it?'

As he pulled a pen from his shirt pocket, Norman told Jesse, 'As a security precaution, I want you to continue your work as a Public Relations officer with the police department, okay? You can moonlight here. After dark, it gets pretty deserted around here, so there'd be ample opportunity to run tests. We'll be functioning as a team, but I am your immediate superior. You'll have to get used to taking orders from me.'

Jesse was still entranced by the motorcycle. His desire to ride the machine overcame his scepticism and any other reservations he might have still had about the project and his involvement with it. 'Okay, Norman,' he said, scribbling his name at the bottom of the contract. 'Here's your contract. Now when can I get my knee worked on so I'll be able to take this baby here for a spin?'

'What's your status at the Police Department . . . in terms of a work schedule, that is.'

'I'm doing a basic nine to five stint,' Jesse divulged. 'Monday through Friday.'

'You'll need at least a couple of days for the surgery and recovery once you've gotten the prosthesis. If you can swing a Monday or Friday off sometime soon, I can schedule you to have things taken care of over that weekend.'

'Well, there's not going to be a better time than this weekend coming up,' Jesse said. 'Can you arrange it that soon?'

Norman nodded as he slipped the contract back in his attaché case and tried to seem nonchalant about the coup he'd just managed. 'Consider it done. If I can get you in by Friday morning, you should be back on your feet in time to go back to work the following Monday afternoon, okay?'

'That's fine by me,' Jesse said, patting the bike's seat. 'The sooner I can get into the saddle on this thing, the happier I'm going to be.'

'It's good to hear you say that, Jesse. With a good attitude, we should be able to see this project through to our mutual satisfaction.'

Jesse leaned forward as if he were passing secrets along to his wounded knee. 'Well, you'd better fasten your seat belt, friend, 'cause you're going back under the knife real soon . . .'

FIFTEEN

The surgery on Jesse's knee was performed at a private clinic affiliated with FILE-TD by way of the Central Intelligence Agency. For all the intricacies involved in the operation, it took a surprisingly short time to be performed. Jesse was equally amazed by his post-op recovery. He'd been sceptical when Norman had told him how long he would have to be hospitalized, but, as promised, he was able to report to work at the police station the following Monday. His knee was still encased in protective wrapping, so it was too soon for him to gauge the success of the prosthesis. He went about his duties with the same limp he had following the incident in the desert and drew no suspicions, aside from Sandy McCoy, who was taken aback by the transformation that had overcome Jesse.

'You're almost being pleasant,' she wisecracked as she dropped by his office near the end of the day. 'I'm not sure what turned you around, but it's a pleasure to see you in this kind of mood.'

'What a difference a weekend can make,' Jesse answered, accepting the armload of materials Sandy had brought for him. 'Any order in which you want me to handle all this?'

'Give the golf tournament top priority, and use your judgement on the rest.'

'Will do.'

Sandy was halfway out of the office when she caught a glimpse of someone walking down the hallway. 'Oh, Freddie!' she called out. 'Could you come in here for just a minute?'

Freddie Williams looked a preppy poster boy in his argyle sweater vest and matching socks. His hair was cut short and the large, round frames of his eyeglasses rested on pudgy cheeks, giving him an owlish countenance. He was carrying a clipboard with visible pride, the way a matador might carry a red cape prior to the commencement of a well-attended bullfight.

'Yes, Ms McCoy?'

'Freddie, I'd like you to meet Jesse Mach. He's the latest addition to the staff here. Jesse, meet Freddie Williams.'

Jesse stood up and extended a hand to his new acquaintance. 'Hiya, Freddie. I've seen you around.'

'Same here, Jesse,' Freddie said, shaking hands. 'I'm sorry about the circumstances that put you here, but I look forward to working with you.'

Sandy excused herself, but Freddie lingered behind in the office. As he sat back down, Jesse said, 'So, Freddie, how do you like PR work?'

'I find it challenging, in my own way. Of course, it's nothing compared to some of the things you've done, I'm sure.' Freddie glanced out into the hallway to make sure no one was eavesdropping, then confided, 'I want you to know that I was betting on you at that harbour jump.'

'A man after my own heart.'

'Well, I gotta get on the horn and make a few calls,' Freddie said. 'If you ever have any questions or need a hand with something, I'm just down the hall. Room twenty.'

'I'll remember that, Freddie. Thanks.'

Once he was alone, Jesse turned his back to the door and reached down to his left leg, gently massaging the wrapped left knee. He couldn't wait for a chance to test it out and see if the prosthesis was working up to expectations. At this stage, much as he yearned to be able to get back on a motorcycle, he would be grateful just for the chance to walk again without the aid of a cane.

After work, Jesse drove back to the warehouse district, where Norman was waiting for him at his camouflaged facilities.

'How's it feeling?' Norman asked as they entered the main enclosure.

'So far so good. The doctors said I can take the brace and top layer of bandages off tonight so I can check things out.'

'I know,' Norman said.

'So when do you think I'll be able to take Street Hawk out on the road?'

'Don't get ahead of yourself, Jesse,' Norman advised. 'I'll be the judge of when you're ready, and I'll tell you up front that you've got a good three weeks of physiotherapy to go through before I'm even going to let you sit on Street Hawk.'

'Three weeks?' Jesse moaned. 'Why so long? Where am I supposed to have this therapy?'

'Right here.' Norman inserted a plastic card into a slot next to a side doorway, then motioned for Jesse to enter a small side room when the door swished open on its hydraulic rollers. The room turned out to be a completely furnished exercise area, with a pair of lockers and adjacent shower facilities.

'The surprises just keep on coming, don't they?'

'I've been using this room to keep in shape myself,' Norman divulged as he handed the plastic card to Jesse. 'Today I had a few new pieces of equipment brought in, though. They've been specially designed to build up that knee of yours.'

'Wonderful.' Jesse sat down on a rowing machine and smirked at all the other contraptions surrounding him. 'When does Jane Fonda get here?'

'She doesn't.' Norman threw open one of the locker doors and tossed a sweatsuit to Jesse. 'Now get started. You have a lot to do. That chart on the wall lists all the exercises you're supposed to do.'

Jesse got up and walked over to the chart. 'Hey, there's enough stuff down here to get me in shape for a decathlon, for crying out loud!'

'Precisely,' Norman said on his way out of the room. 'Street Hawk's in the finest working order. If you want to ride it, you're going to have to match it.'

As Norman left the room and hissed the door shut behind him, Jesse slowly began to change. Under his breath he muttered, 'Something tells me I should have read the small print on that contract before I signed it...'

SIXTEEN

Jesse found a way to get Jane Fonda to join him for his workouts. He tracked down a poster promoting her latest fitness video and bought it off a bribeable sales clerk, then taped it up in the exercise room. Not that he was in desperate need of incentives for going through with the arduous physical regimen Norman and the doctors had prescribed for him. Although every muscle in his body ached with protest after his first day of exercise, Jesse's ability to flex his knee gave him due cause to endure the pain and come back the following evening with firm resolve to maintain the discipline required to make his therapy successful. Norman was there to provide additional encouragement as well, dropping in periodically when he needed a breather from his own exhaustive work on the final preparations for Operation Street Hawk. During one such visit, Norman found Jesse straining to complete a leg-lift.

'Jesse, you're not supposed to start on those until the end of the week! No shortcuts, do you understand?'

Jesse's face was gleaming with sweat and flushed red with the strain of trying to hoist his bad leg. Finally, with one supreme effort, he was able to lift the leg up into the air. It trembled in space for a few seconds, then slammed back down on the padded bench he was lying on. Between breaths, Jesse gasped, 'Just checking, Norman. Did you see that?'

'Yes, I saw it,' Norman snapped irritably, 'and if I see it again before you're scheduled to do it, there's going to be trouble!'

'But I feel great!' Jesse protested.

'Good, let's make sure to keep it that way! Now, no more

leg-lifts until I clear you to do 'em! That's an order!'

By the end of the following week, Jesse was singing another tune, as was Norman. According to Jesse's workout chart, he was supposed to be doing thirteen leg-lifts, but by the time he'd completed his sixth, Jesse looked as if he was ready to collapse.

'I... can't do... any more!'

'That's six,' Norman counted, leaning over Jesse like a ruthless PE instructor. 'Seven more... come on!'

Jesse shook his head. 'C-c-c-can't!'

'Get 'em up, Mach!' Norman barked. 'You're almost halfway home! Quit sandbagging!'

With an anguished grunt, Jesse strained his legs upward. 'I'll kill you, Tuttle!' he threatened.

'Seven!' Norman cheered. 'Keep it up.'

'I'll crush you into little pieces and put you on my breakfast!' Jesse seethed as he struggled through another repetition.

'Eight! Go ahead and shoot your mouth off if you think it'll help. Five more!'

'Your mother wears motorcross boots!'

'Nine!'

Jesse felt as if someone were adding weights to his ankles. He thought that any second his prosthesis was going to snap from over-use. Glaring through his sweat at Norman, he continued to rage, 'You... get a... big kick... out of watching me... suffer...'

Norman grinned with mock sadism. 'That's ten, Mach. You're in the home stretch!'

'Eleven!' Jesse howled, tightening his buttocks as he pulled his legs up one more time. Then, rather than taking a long pause to gather more strength, he kept up his momentum and swung his feet up the moment after they had touched the padding of his bench. 'Twelve!'

Jesse completed one final pump, then rolled limply off the bench and onto the carpeted floor, groaning like a man too fatigued to go through the death throes that his body seemed to be calling for. He was perspiring from head to toe, and once he blinked the sweat from his eyes, he glanced up to the poster of Jane Fonda and whispered weakly, 'I went for the burn. I hope you're happy . . .'

'I'm thrilled, Jesse.' Norman stepped in front of the poster and leaned over the fallen man, handing him a towel. 'Just think, next week you'll be able to work up to two sessions a day.'

'Huh?'

'That's right. Starting on Monday, I want you in here during your lunch hour.' Jesse buried his face in the towel, sopping up the sweat and muffling his voice as he said, 'That's not on the schedule.'

'I know it's not, but I've talked to the doctors about your progress with the knee, and they feel that if you double up your therapy workouts, we can push up the testing schedule a week.'

Jesse tossed aside the towel and struggled to his feet. 'Why didn't you say so in the first place?' He took a few small steps, circling the workout bench. His knee was wrapped with only one layer of elastic bandage, but it was still capable of supporting his weight when he walked on it. The limp that had been so prominent in his step before was far less pronounced. He was able to get around without the cane.

'Very good, Jesse,' Norman commented.

'Fred Astaire, watch out!'

SEVENTEEN

Given the green light by Sandy McCoy to establish his own priorities with regard to his workload, Jesse was able to compile an extensive list of errands and business calls that took him away from the office much of every day. Further, he was able to juggle his time on the road in such a way that he was able to squeeze in an extended midday workout at Street Hawk headquarters. He owed the success of this routine in part to Freddie Williams, who was more than glad to swap various tasks with Jesse. Freddie preferred to remain at the office, so he could avoid having to interrupt his work just to fight LA traffic.

Sandy was willing at first to tolerate Jesse's prolonged absences, mostly because she realized she had unwittingly sanctioned his right to be away from the office. But as the week wore on, she became increasingly agitated about the situation, and by Friday she finally found an excuse to vent her anger.

After checking Jesse's office and finding him gone, she stormed down the hallway and dropped in on Freddie, who was camped out on the phone. He gestured that he'd be through in a moment, and Sandy waited impatiently for him to finish his call, drumming her fingers on the doorframe.

'Okay, Vince, that'll about do it. I'll touch base with you again on Monday to firm things up, okay? Right . . . bye, and have a good weekend.' Freddie hung up the phone and turned to Sandy, sensing her irritation immediately. 'What's up?'

'Freddie, have you seen Jesse?'

'I think he had to leave early, Ms McCoy. He mentioned something about checking on the promo posters for the golf tournament. Why, is anything wrong?'

'Plenty!' Sandy steamed. 'He never dropped off those press releases on the department promotions at the mayor's office! Mayor Southe wanted them for his press conference this afternoon . . . twenty minutes from now, as a matter of fact!'

Freddie knew very well that Jesse wasn't out checking on any promotion posters, and he suspected his newfound friend had probably forgotten all about the press releases. Thinking fast, he forced a chuckle as he gathered a few papers into his briefcase and stood up. 'If the truth be known, Ms McCoy, I was just on my way to drop off those press releases myself. You see, I've got some business with Mrs Flannagan at the City Commission office and I figured I might as well kill two birds with one stone.'

Thwarted, all Sandy could do was stand aside to let Freddie by. As he started off down the hallway, she fumed, 'Mr Mach's been working here for almost two weeks now and I hardly ever see him! For all I know, he could be sunning himself at the beach and letting a troupe of elves do all his work for him!'

On his way to Jesse's office at the end of the hall, Freddie called back to Sandy, 'Last time I checked, it didn't look like Jesse was getting a tan to me. For that matter, I think he's been doing a lot better work than the last guy we had . . .' Taking the press releases, Freddie retreated inside the elevator before Sandy could respond, and he grinned at himself with satisfaction for having come to Jesse's defence. Instead of pushing for the basement garage, he signalled for the fourth floor, which housed the department's Internal Affairs division. As expected, Freddie ran into Jesse in the hallway, where he was talking to another officer.

'Excuse me, Jesse, but I need a quick word with you.'

'Just a sec.' Jesse wrapped up his conversation with the other man, then turned back to Freddie. 'You look like there's trouble . . .'

'A close call.' Freddie quickly relayed Sandy's fit of temper, then handed Jesse the press releases. 'I knew you were up here, so I covered for you, but I can't drop these off at City Hall for you. Sorry.'

'That's okay, I'll do it. Listen, thanks a lot for going to bat for me, Freddie. Nice to know somebody around here's on my side.'

'So you didn't have any luck here?'

Jesse checked up and down the hallway, then shook his head. 'Nothing. Look, I'll tell you about it later. Right now I better run with this stuff for the mayor.'

Jesse was having a battle with his own temper, and it took a feat of willpower for him to hold it in check while he made the delivery to City Hall and traded niceties with the mayor's secretary. By then it was close enough to five o'clock for Jesse to decide there was no need to return to the station, especially if there was a chance he'd run into Sandy. The last thing he needed to do in his frame of mind was to lock horns with someone spoiling for a fight.

When he showed up at Street Hawk headquarters, Jesse found Norman rewiring one of the computer panels on his command module. Norman glanced up from his work and frowned, 'What's the matter? You look fit to be tied, Jesse.'

'I did a little snooping up at Internal Affairs today,' Jesse related as he jerked his tie off and unbuttoned the collar of his dress shirt. 'I wanted to see how it was going with their investigation into what happened in the desert. I managed to sneak a look at Marty's file, and they hadn't even got around to filing a preliminary report. No lab workups . . . nothing.'

'I'm sure there's a logical explanation,' Norman theorized as he went back to work on the computer panel with a soldering gun.

'Yeah, somebody's sitting on the case, that's the logical explanation,' Jesse snapped hotly. 'I want to find out why!'

'Well, you're not going to find out right now.' Norman soldered his connection, then set down the soldering gun and started putting the panel back in place. 'How's the knee?'

'It takes a licking but keeps on ticking,' Jesse said.

'Good. Why don't you suit up and take out some of that frustration on the Nautiles machine . . .'

EIGHTEEN

By the time Jesse had finished his exercises, showered, and changed back into his street clothes, Norman had completed his latest round of modifications and was now working on Street Hawk itself. Jesse came over and circled around the bike as he had numerous times before, admiring the sleek, graceful design and the aura of power the machine seemed to exude even without being turned on.

'How many times have you taken this baby out for a spin, Norman?'

'"This baby", as you call it, has never been riden before.' Norman stood up and eyed Jesse squarely. 'I assumed you knew that. Why do you think you were brought in on this project, anyway?'

'But if no one's ever even ridden it, how do you know if it works?'

Norman sighed and walked away from the bike, telling Jesse, 'Here, let me show you something.'

They went over to the control module, where Norman punched up a revolving three-dimensional schematic of Street Hawk.

'Computers,' Jesse said. 'You've got it all figured out on computers, right?'

'That's it, yes,' Norman confirmed. 'After all, the basic design and principles of operation are much the same as they are for any other bike, so there's no question about it being rideable. With the input of the latest technology, we've been able to attend to a few areas that will provide the bike with some additional functions ... not to mention improving the existing variables such as design impact on drag, shock suspension and whatnot...'

'I'm all ears,' Jesse said, staring intently at the screen. 'Tell me more. I'll let you know if you're going over my head.'

Referring to the schematic already on the screen, Norman went on, 'Okay, then... as far as design goes, Street Hawk was built so that it has an aerodynamic drag coefficient of 0.05. Friction is practically nonexistent, or at least non-traceable.'

'Without a rider, of course,' Jesse interjected.

'Of course.' Norman cued up a profile shot of the bike, then zoomed in for a tighter view. 'It's also equipped with a hydraulic suspension system that adjusts to either street or off-road use.'

Responding to keyboard commands from Norman, the schematic on the screen demonstrated the low mode for street riding and the higher suspension cushion required for off-road operation. Jesse watched with rapt attention, taking it all in as Norman ran through a briefing on the bike's fuel and lubrication systems. Then they returned to the actual bike itself, and Norman pointed out the newly developed drive system.

'Tricky, Norman,' Jesse said, taking a close look. 'Really tricky.'

'Thanks. I spent four months alone getting the bugs out of that.' Norman shifted his focus to the engine compartment. Pointing, he resumed, 'And these attachments are –'.

'High volume air boxes,' Jesse guessed. 'They boost your horsepower.'

'*Your* horsepower, when the time comes, Jesse.'

'Right.' Jesse fingered the boxes, then tested the throttle. 'Tell me, Norman, just how fast does she go?'

'Again, it's never been driven, so we can only speculate. According to the computers, its estimated cruising speed is two hundred miles per hour.'

'Whoah, are you kidding me?!! That's a lot of juice.'

Norman shrugged. 'With hyperthrust, it should be able to approach three hundred.'

'Three hundred miles an hour on a motorcycle?' Jesse was dumbfounded. 'We're talking a two-wheeled jet here,

Norman.'

'Perhaps . . .'

'What's this hyperthrust?'

'A computer-assist mode that I control,' Norman replied.

'Wait a minute.' Jesse was confused. 'I thought I was the test pilot here . . .'

Norman had anticipated this confrontation some time ago, and in the face of its inevitability he'd spent considerable time thinking through a tactful way of laying down operational ground rules for the use of the motorcyle. 'Jesse, Street Hawk is just too complex a piece of machinery for one man to handle to its fullest potential. It's a two-man bike.'

'Don't be ridiculous,' Jesse protested. 'You put two riders on that cycle and you've cancelled out just about every technological goody you've –'

'I didn't say anything about *riding* with you.' Norman pointed over at the master command module. 'I'm tied in by close-circuit video and audio. If Street Hawk or you malfunction in any way, I can immediately shut down the bike and hopefully avoid any disaster.'

Jesse didn't care much for the arrangement and made no effort to hide his displeasure. 'Just what I need,' he grumbled, 'a backseat driver.'

'That's the way it's going to be, so you might as well get used to it. Now stand back so I can show you a few other things.' Once Jesse was out of the way, Norman reached over the bike and squeezed hard on the hand brake. The side airfoils suddenly snapped out of their housings and locked into position. Norman explained, 'For maximum braking power, I've redesigned these airfoils to take full advantage of negative air flow. If necessary, you'll be able literally to stop on a dime. I don't need to tell you how careful you have to be on a manoeuvre like that . . .'

Jesse nodded as he moved closer to inspect the left handle. Noticing a small lever, he reached for it. 'What's this thing do?'

Norman swatted Jesse's hand away before he could grab the lever. 'That controls the compressed air vertical lift system.'

'The what?'

'Touch that lever while you're driving and a blast of compressed air will propel you approximately thirty metres in the air . . . without having to ride up a ramp, mind you.'

'Wow!' Jesse was genuinely impressed. 'I'd be able to leap tall buildings with a single bound, huh?'

'Possibly . . . but I forbid you to wear that insufferable cape and helmet you had on for that harbour jump of yours.'

Jesse laughed and gave Norman a playful jab on the shoulder. 'Hey, so you have a sense of humour after all!'

Norman tried his best to suppress a smile, but his lips rebelled against him and he grinned at the compliment. 'Not all engineers are stuffed shirts, you know. Okay, I think that's enough of a briefing for one night. I'm going to shut things –'

'Wait, Norman . . .' Jesse was staring hard at the bike, letting his eyes trail from the brake system to the compressor lever. 'What would happen if I hit vertical lift, then jammed on the airfoils?'

Norman thought it through, then said, 'Theoretically, the bike would do a mid-air back loop and you'd probably kill yourself, so don't even think about it, okay?'

'Too bad,' Jesse sighed. 'Sounds like fun.'

As he headed for the control module, Norman said, 'We'll go into the attack and defence modes tomorrow night maybe.'

Seeing that Norman's back was turned, Jesse gave in to a long-standing temptation and leapt onto Street Hawk. Almost instantaneously the bike seemed to come to life. A dull hum sounded from beneath the seat and grew both louder and more shrill. As Jesse opened his mouth to shout something, the seat suddenly sprang up to a ninety degree angle, unceremoniously hurling its rider over the handlebars. Jesse had taken enough falls from dirt bikes in his time, so he was able to cushion his fall by tumbling head over heels, but he was still stunned.

'What did I do?' he said as Norman stared at him.

'Nothing,' Norman said. 'I just haven't programmed the bike for you yet.'

As he rose to his feet, Jesse eyed the bike with newfound respect. 'Boy, that's some alarm system.'

As they were leaving the warehouse, Norman carefully noted the way Jesse was walking. Before Jesse could get into his Mustang, Norman called out, 'Wait!'

'What is it, Norman?'

'I'm glad your knee's getting better so quickly,' Norman said as he opened the rear door of his station wagon and swung it up, 'but I'm going to have to ask you to go back to wearing this brace when you're not here. I don't want anyone suspecting it's you when Operation Street Hawk commences.'

Jesse eyed the brace with aversion when Norman held it out to him. 'Is that really necessary?'

'I'm afraid so. The limp will throw people off.'

Jesse made a sour face as he pulled up his pant leg high enough so that he could apply the brace over the bandage on his rebuilt knee. 'I still don't see why this project is so top secret.'

'Because some people might not like the idea of an attack motorcycle patrolling their streets,' Norman said. 'We don't want this project stopped before it gets off the ground. Once Street Hawk has been fully tested, a decision will be made as to whether or not we offer it to local law enforcement. Someday, Jesse, my dream is to have a Street Hawk in every police garage across the country.'

'And how about a chicken in every pot while you're at it?' Jesse finished adjusting the brace, then lowered the pant leg and stood up. Norman gave him his cane back and Jesse took a few practice steps, affecting his former limp. 'I'll play along with you on this, up to a point. How long is it going to take to get the operation off the ground, Norman? I didn't sign up for life, you know.'

Norman got into his station wagon and started it up. 'It will take as long as it takes,' he told Jesse. 'And as a matter of fact, you *did* sign up for life . . .'

As Norman drove off, Jesse stared numbly at the retreating rear lights of the station wagon. 'For life . . . ?'

NINETEEN

Instead of going home, Jesse drove back to the police station, determined to follow through on his own personal investigation into the desert ambush that had left his best friend slain. Next to Marty and Mike Holt, Jesse's best friend on the force was Ernie Cerga, a former pro relief pitcher who now did desk duty at the station's impound centre. He was in his mid-forties, with traces of white and grey beginning to infiltrate the curls of his well-groomed afro. When he saw Jesse slip in the side door and approach his desk, Ernie flashed a smile.

'Hey, dude! It's been a while...'

'How's it goin', Ernie?' Jesse shook hands with the officer.

'I'm hangin' in there, Jess. Yourself?'

'About the same. Listen, Ernie. I need to ask you a favour... something under the table.'

Ernie cocked an eyebrow and rubbed his moustache with the back of his hand. 'Fire away, friend. You know I still owe you from that time over on Seventh Street.' Ernie was referring to an altercation three years ago that had put an end to his career on the street. He'd taken a bullet in the shoulder from a liquor store bandit and was within a split second of taking a second shot to the head when Jesse had arrived on the scene and leapt the kerb on his patrol cycle, bowling over the thug before he could pull the trigger.

'I want to take a look at my bike and Marty's,' Jesse explained. 'I assume they were brought here from the desert.'

'Hmm, you know, I don't remember seeing any paperwork on that, as a matter of fact. Let me do a quick rundown on it, though.'

'Thanks, Ernie. I appreciate it.'

Ernie swung around in his chair and banged away on the keyboard of a small computer. The monitor screen flashed on as Ernie called up the date the bikes would have been brought into the station for impoundment. 'That's odd,' he said. 'I don't have a record of it. Let me try the next day . . .'

When that still failed to produce any information, Ernie punched into the interdepartmental computer network and tried to see if there was any pertinent data at any other impound centres in the area.

'Negative, Jesse.'

'It has to be here!' Jesse said. 'IA has the case. All the evidence should have been tagged and logged in.'

'What can I tell you?' Ernie shrugged his shoulders. 'If it's not on the computers, I have no way of tracking it down.'

Jesse wasn't about to be deterred. He asked, 'Ernie, you gotta let me have a look around the lot. I know the bikes have to be around here somewhere.'

Ernie glanced at the clock on the wall across from him. 'Well, we're between shifts in another ten minutes. If you can wait until then, you could have a few minutes to sniff around before the graveyard crew comes on.'

'Great. I'll go for it. Thanks, Ernie.'

'Glad to help, bro.'

Jesse spent most of the ten minutes back at his car, tracking down a flashlight in his trunk and donning an old pair of battered sneakers in place of his Florsheims. At eleven o'clock sharp, he returned to the impound area and waited for Ernie to flash him a signal before slipping through the gate that led to the storage area. He quickly bypassed the inside cubicles containing pieces of evidence that could be stored on shelves and made his way to the back lot, which was choked with automobiles, large appliances, trailers, and other big objects that looked very sinister in the dim light of an overhead lamp. Blinking his flashlight on from time to time, Jesse hurriedly scanned the various aisles, discerning shapes in an instant and moving on when they didn't resemble what he was looking for. A full five minutes had passed before he found the two bikes stashed away in a back corner, wedged between a stolen panel truck and a dialysis machine carefully wrapped in a layer of thick plastic.

'I knew they'd be here,' Jesse whispered to himself as he squatted for a closer look at the bikes. He realized that he didn't have much time left, so he quickly focused the beam of his flashlight on the crumpled sections of each bike that marked where they had been struck by the pickup. He couldn't find any potential evidence on his bike, but on Marty's Yamaha there was a telltale black gash on the crushed gas tank. Using his car keys, Jesse scraped off a few flecks of the dark paint and folded them inside a public relations envelope he happened to have in his back pocket.

Turning off his flashlight, Jesse was on his way back to the gate when he heard voices in the lot. The late night shift had come on duty, blocking his way out of the impound area. Hiding behind the panel truck, Jesse listened intently to the voices, hoping he'd recognize Ernie's unmistakable accent. He didn't.

Deciding that he would have to find an alternative way out, Jesse looked behind him at the fence that surrounded the lot. Eight feet of cyclone fencing was topped by coils of barbed wire, making it virtually impossible to climb over. However, he noticed that a tree on the other side of the fence had one of its lower limbs stretching to within a few yards of the barbed wire. There was a chance that by climbing to the top of the panel truck and vaulting over the top of the fence, he could catch hold of the branch to break his fall. It was his best, perhaps only chance, so he quietly rolled up his pant leg one more time and removed the knee brace to give him better mobility. After waiting until he was sure the guards were on the other side of the lot, he quickly scaled the side of the panel truck, then paused to catch his breath before making the jump. He came within a couple of inches of snagging his pants on the barbed wire, but managed to clear the fence and grab hold of the branch, which supported his weight. The tree rustled slightly, but there was a breeze, and no attention was drawn his way. After dropping to the ground, Jesse stole furtively back to his Mustang and drove off.

TWENTY

Jesse wasn't through begging favours from other friends on the force. Monday morning he stopped off at the trace lab, located a few doors down from ballistics. His lab connection was Bernie Goldberg, a hyperactive fussbudget with a beard as full as his head was bare. In his white smock, he whirled about the lab as if he were in the process of inventing the latest dance craze, tending to two assignments while simultaneously listening to Jesse's request for help. Before Jesse even had a chance to finish his appeal, Bernie cut in, holding a large glass jar in his hands and staring at its contents with unbridled contempt.

'See this? See this? You know what this is?'

Jesse was familiar with Bernie's high-strung nature and took the man's outburst in his stride. Looking at the object in Bernie's hand, he said, 'Seems to me it's a mayonnaise jar full of dirt.'

'Exactly!' From the exultation in Bernie's voice, one would have thought Jesse had just confirmed a discovery that would ensure them the Nobel Prize. However, his excitement quickly took on a harsh edge and he complained, 'They expect me to find bomb fragments in this schmootz, if you can believe that. This is after the lousy fire department comes in and Pinesol's the entire street, mind you. This dirt here is cleaner than my bathroom. You see what I'm up against, Jesse?'

Jesse nodded, then sighed, 'Bernie, can you help me or not?'

For all his surface abrasiveness, Bernie Goldberg was basically a pushover. Setting down the mayonnaise jar, he stuffed his hands in the pockets of his smock and asked Jesse, 'What have you got?'

'Paint chips.' Jesse pulled the envelope from his pants pocket and handed it to Bernie, who unfolded it enough to peek at the contents. 'I need a full analysis, Bernie.'

'Are you kidding?' Bernie launched into his final argument, waving his free hand at the surrounding clutter of the lab. 'Look at this mess, wouldya? I'm backed up to my tonsils!'

'Bernie, it's important. Come on, you went through the academy with Marty and me. How about a little loyalty?'

Bernie Goldberg responded to the prospect of guilt the way Pavlov's dogs responded to dinner bells. 'All right, all right, all right!' He threw his arms up in surrender and went fitfully back to his other projects. 'I'll try to get to it when I come back from lunch. No promises, though, understand?'

'I know you'll get to it as soon as you can, Bernie.' Jesse patted his friend on the back, then headed out the door. 'Thanks. I owe you.'

Bernie rolled his eyes. 'Everybody owes me. If you all paid up, I could retire!'

Rather than take the elevator, Jesse used the stairwell to hustle back down to the ground floor. As he emerged into the main hallway, he was besieged by a pair of scrambling sixth grade boys who were barrelling down the hallway as if they were sprinting at tryouts for the Junior Olympics.

'Paul! Robert! Get back here!' a teacher called out from the opposite end of the hallway, where she had her hands full trying to keep the rest of her herd from bolting. Sandy McCoy was with the teacher, and when she spotted Jesse, her eyes narrowed to angry slits.

'Freeze!' Jesse told the boys as he grabbed them, one under each arm, and carried them back to the rest of their classmates. 'You're under arrest.'

'No!' one of the boys squealed playfully as he tried in vain to wriggle free. 'We'll be good! Promise!'

As he set the boys down, Jesse beamed at the other children. 'Hi, kids. You must be my nine o'clock tour. You're early.'

'No, you're late!' Sandy retorted as she stepped in front of the children and confronted Jesse. 'I want a word with you.'

'Oh boy,' Jesse groaned. 'I can hardly wait...'

Sandy excused herself to the teacher, then moved across the hall to an alcove rammed with vending machines. Standing squarely before Jesse, she lectured, 'I take a lot of pride in my department, Officer Mach. I feel it's just as important as any other division in this entire police department. And I'm getting very tired of you treating it like a second job. Now, if you don't have a real good excuse for being everywhere but your desk since you've started here, I'm going to file a formal complaint with Commander Altobelli and Commissioner Miller!'

'It's personal,' Jesse shot back. 'Besides, I seem to recall you saying that as long as I took care of that Celebrity Golf Tournament, which I did, I could set my own schedule as far as –'

'I gave you an inch and you took a mile,' Sandy accused. 'I won't accept that as an excuse. You'll have to come up with something better!'

Jesse wasn't in the mood for an interrogation. He matched Sandy's perturbed glare with a scowl of his own. 'In case you've forgotten, Ms McCoy, my best friend was murdered in an ambush out in the desert a couple of weeks ago, and I nearly cashed in my chips, too. You want to know something else? Somebody around here wants to sweep that whole episode under the rug, and I'm not going to let it happen. I owe it to Marty and I owe it to me! So excuse me if I take a little time off now and then to look into things, but it's more important to me than haggling with printers over the price of printing up tickets for the Policemen's Ball! Okay?'

Sandy was surprised by the intensity of Jesse's comeback, and it took her several prolonged seconds to regain her composure. When she did, much of the anger was gone from her voice, replaced by a trace of concern. 'That's a very serious accusation about the investigation, Officer Mach. Do you have any proof?'

'Not yet, but I'm working on it.'

'I can appreciate your situation,' Sandy told him, 'but you

have to remember that you're not a street cop any more. You work in Public Relations now. Let the proper authorities handle the investigation; we handle the public and the press. That's it. I'm sorry . . .'

'When I first reported to you, Ms McCoy, I seem to remember you telling me that you got your start in journalism. Isn't that right?'

'Yes, but I don't see what that has to do with anything.'

'It has everything to do with it,' Jesse insisted. 'Doesn't getting to the truth matter to you any more? Are you so damn caught up waving your little Public Relations flag that you refuse to consider that something wrong's going on around here? Think about it, would you?'

Jesse stormed off, leaving Sandy staring at the vending machines, stunned.

TWENTY-ONE

Roughly five miles from the site where Jesse had nearly lost his life, a handful of large country estates thrived off a lavish supply of water diverted from the sprawling aqueduct that extended from the central part of the state all the way south to Los Angeles. Surrounded by the parched and semi-barren wilderness of the desert, this cloistered enclave was filled with greenery, from acres of well-trimmed lawns and plots of landscaped gardens to the cottonwoods and drooping poplars that lined the streets. This was a rich man's paradise, and the cars that prowled its freshly-paved avenues were all leisure vehicles costing as much as some middle-class homes. Rolls-Royces, Bentleys, Jaguars, BMWs, Cadillacs – they basked in driveways like polished gems on four wheels.

Out on the street, one particular Mercedes, a vintage '71 28OSE with a grey body and black top, drove slowly past mansion after mansion until it came to a lot that was hidden behind a tall stone wall half-covered with creeping fig. A remote closed-circuit television peered out through the bars of a wrought iron gate as the Mercedes pulled into the driveway and slowed to a halt. A few moments later, the gates slowly parted and the Mercedes proceeded forward. The driveway wound through a wooded area for almost a hundred yards, then opened out into a clearing, upon which had been built a large, two-storey Tudor home, flanked on one side by a stately oak tree that was easily the oldest living resident in the entire development. A handful of other luxury cars were parked alongside the house, as was an unmistakable black off-road pickup truck. The Mercedes parked next to a metallic DeLorean resting under the shade of the oak. When the driver's door of the 28OSE opened, Police Commissioner Thomas Miller climbed out and straightened his suit before closing the door and striding uncertainly around to the back yard.

An Olympic-sized pool was the centrepiece of an ornately designed recreation area taking up much of the back yard. Chaise longues were set about the pool's periphery. Most of them were occupied by nubile young women in scanty swimsuits who stretched out lethargically under the lulling rays of the sun, giving off the pungent odour of tanning lotion and fruit daquiris. A few men stood off to one side, huddling under a wide-spanning umbrella as they murmured over their drinks. In the pool, Anthony Corrido was swimming laps while, off in the shallow end, a young blonde waded drunkenly towards him, slurring her words as she sang a song that only she could understand. The water grew progressively deeper around her, and with each step she seemed less sure-footed. Finally she stopped singing and slumped backwards, slipping beneath the waterline. As Commissioner Miller watched on with a combination of dread and revulsion, Corrido swam over and dragged the woman to the edge of the pool, where two bodyguards in Brooks Brothers suits leaned over to pull her up out of the water. Miller was close enough to see the drugged look in the young woman's eyes as the gazed blearily at her saviours.

'She couldn't take the heat,' Corrido told the Commissioner as he climbed out of the pool and reached for a towel. He was in incredible shape, with the wide, muscular shoulders of a committed swimmer.

'I got your call this morning,' Miller told the other man. 'I came as soon as I could. Your message said it was urgent.'

'It is.' Once he had finished towelling himself off, Corrido walked over to a nearby picnic table and poured himself a drink from a tall pitcher of chilled lemonade. 'Thirsty?' he asked Miller.

'No thanks... well, maybe I will, after all.' The Commissioner's throat was dry and tight. He'd never cared much for his dealings with Corrido, but things had progressed to the point where he no longer felt it was in his power to cut off the relationship. He knew only too well the possible consequences of snubbing Anthony Corrido.

After Corrido had handed Miller a drink and they had both downed healthy sips of the lemonade, Corrido asked, 'Have you set up the next shipment yet?'

'I have to be careful,' Miller insisted, guarding his words. 'It's still too close to the last one. We don't want to blow this thing by getting greedy.'

Corrido laughed, but there was little amusement in the outburst. 'Check the layout here, Commissioner. I didn't get this way be being timid. There's nothing wrong with a little greed, as long as you're smart about it.'

'That's exactly my point. It's not smart to jump ahead with another –'

'You have a week to set it up.'

'But that's impossible!' Miller gasped. 'You can't be serious. There's no way I can do that!'

'You can do it if you want to,' Corrido said. 'I mean, after all, you're the Commissioner, right?'

'It's not that easy, Corrido.' Miller finished his lemonade but it did little to soothe the knot in his throat. He pleaded, 'You don't understand. There's still a lot of heat from last time. They're apt to beef up security if and when they make another run –'

'That's why we're going to move fast . . . before they can set up any fancy new delivery arrangements. Kapish?'

Miller saw that it was pointless to argue further. He set down his glass. 'I'll see what I can do.'

'You do that. Now, what's happening with Jesse Mach?'

'He's been asking a few questions around the department, but it's nothing to be concerned about.'

'But I *am* concerned, Commissioner.'

Miller fished through his pocket for his car keys. 'I can handle it,' he assured Corrido.

Just then another of Corrido's playmates staggered toward him, almost tripping over one of the chaise longues. She was a redhead with matching sunglasses and a swimsuit that looked like spare parts for a slingshot. 'Baby, I'm really feeling sick,' she cooed playfully as she reached Corrido and began fondling his shoulders. 'I need some more medicine.'

The Commissioner took a step back, struggling to keep a straight face. A part of him deplored what he was witnessing, but he also knew that under different circumstances, he'd be playing along with Corrido's women. 'I have to get back,' he said.

Corrido put his arm around the redhead as he grinned at Miller. 'I'll be waiting for your call.'

As the Commissioner turned and walked away, the redhead continued to whine in Corrido's ear. '*Please* Tony? Oh, baby, I really, really need it . . .'

'Get away from me!' Corrido pried himself loose from the woman and strode off to where the two bodyguards were standing in the nearest shade. 'Jimmy . . .' he beckoned the shorter of the men.

'Yes, sir?'

'I want Jesse Mach dead. Take care of it.'

Jimmy's expression remained unchanged as he nodded his head at Corrido. 'Yes, sir . . .'

TWENTY-TWO

As Jesse sat in the middle of the command centre, Norman approached him from behind, like an archbishop about to crown a king. Instead of a crown, however, he was holding an aerodynamically designed motorcycle helmet. It was the same brooding shade of black as Street Hawk, with a slightly bluish tint to the reflector visor that covered Jesse's entire face once the helmet was placed on his head.

'How does it feel?' Norman asked.

'A perfect fit,' came the muffled response. 'It makes everything else I've ever worn feel like saucepans... and, wow, what a view! Norman, this is amazing!'

The curvature of the visor was such that Jesse's visual field covered a much wider angle than normal. It was almost as if the world were coming to him in Cinemascope. As he sat in place, marvelling over the altered perspective of the room around him, Jesse could see Norman approach the command module and begin fiddling with the controls. Soon a familiar voice was coming to him through small, high-efficiency speakers inside the helmet.

'Okay, now you'll be noticing digital readouts in each corner,' Norman explained. 'The left computes your speed and RPMS. The right calibrates distance.'

'Amazing,' Jesse muttered. 'Saves me the trouble of having to look down at the speedometer.'

'To say the least. Directly below the distance readings is what we call a monocle targeting system. You're also equipped with infra-red detectors and light amplification systems,' Norman went on, 'for all-weather and night fighting capability. Anything you see, I see. And it's all automatically recorded.'

'Is that so?' Smirking behind his visor, Jesse turned slightly and gazed through the plexiglass window of the exercise room, focusing on his beloved poster of Jane Fonda.

'Do you mind?' Norman's voice droned in his ear.

'Sorry,' Jesse said. 'I can see right now that you're going to end up being as bad as my conscience, only louder.'

Norman shut down the command console, then came over and helped Jesse take off the helmet, telling him, 'Now we need to come up with a riding suit to go with this. You're going to have to strip down to your skivvies and step into that tube over there.'

'I beg your pardon?'

'You heard me.'

'That's what I was afraid of. Do I really have to?'

'Come on, Jesse. It's the same thing as being fitted for ski boots, only on a larger scale. Nothing to worry about.'

'That's easy for you to say, Norman.'

Jesse reluctantly undressed, then padded across the room in his undershorts. The tube Norman had mentioned was roughly the shape of an upright coffin and made of clear, thick plastic. As soon as he stepped inside, Norman closed the tube door behind him and clamped its seals tightly. There was an opening in the top of the tube, allowing the two men to converse.

'Okay, now stand at attention and hold your position.'

Jesse obliged, and moments after Norman had triggered a pump switch, a bubbling foam began to rise from the bottom of the tube. As the cold material crept upward, Jesse shivered involuntarily and glanced down. 'Are you sure you know what you're doing, Norman?'

'After all the time we spent cutting down on drag in the motorcycle, the least we can do is make an effort to come up with a suit that will do the same. This will give us an exact body mould to make an outfit from.'

'This must be how they squeeze those fashion models into blue jeans, right?'

'Don't move or we'll have to do it all again!' Norman chided.

Jesse froze in place, but managed to crack a smile. 'I'm sure that somewhere in this town there're people who'd pay money to have this done to them on a regular basis . . .'

Once the foam had risen as high as Jesse's neck, Norman turned off the pump and moved over to Street Hawk. 'That foam's specially formulated to be quick drying, but you're still going to have to stay put for a couple of minutes, so let me brief you on the bike's offensive capabilities.'

Jesse had a clear view of Street Hawk from the tube, and he watched as Norman activated a switch that sprang open a small housing in front of the handlebars. A futuristic-looking weapon pivoted around so that its segmented barrel pointed out over the front wheel.

'I take it that's something besides a fancy radio antenna,' Jesse guessed.

'It's a transmitter capable of emitting high-energy particle beams,' Norman said. 'There are two basic settings. The maximum charge can neutralize a ten-ton truck. With reduced power it can stun and immobilize suspects. I don't have to tell you what would happen if you chose the wrong setting in the wrong situation.'

Jesse whistled slowly, imagining the destructive capabilities he'd have at his command with the weapon. 'Hey, Norman, is Street Hawk equipped with anything a little more, you know, conventional? I mean, I don't think I'm going to be facing World War III every time I go out.'

Norman snapped the left handle grip counterclockwise. A small, tubular-shaped piece of equipment popped out, and Norman held it up for Jesse to see. 'It fires a soft rubber slug. Any more questions?'

'Yeah. When can I get out of here?'

Norman eyed Jesse wickedly and started to walk out of the room, humming nonchalantly to himself.

'Come on, Norman . . . quit messing around . . .'

TWENTY-THREE

Jesse's stomach was growling as he drove down the incline leading to the underground parking lot beneath his apartment complex.

'Down, boy,' he mumbled, patting his belly. He pulled into his assigned parking space, then carefully eased himself out of the Mustang, cursing the need to wear his insufferable knee brace. He would be glad when the whole secretive phase of Operation Street Hawk was completed. Then he could throw off his charade of having a bad knee and convince Altobelli that he was fit enough to rejoin the street force.

Lost in thought, Jesse wasn't aware that he was being watched until the thunderous din of a dirt bike echoed off the concrete walls of the parking structure and he turned to see a single headlight bearing down on him. Behind the glaring beam, he could make out the outline of a rider raising one arm and pointing it at him. Jesse's instincts took over and he quickly dived to one side and crawled between the nearest parked cars.

As the rider of the dirt bike raced by, he fired his wrist cannon, sending an explosive charge crashing into the side of a custom Ferrari. Jesse flattened himself against the concrete as the explosion showered him with shrapnel and hot sparks. He avoided any serious injury, however, and as he sprang back to his feet, he grabbed his fallen cane and quickly weaved through the parked cars, keeping an eye on the dirt biker, who matched the description of the thieves who had ambushed the police van on its way to the harbour a few weeks ago. When the rider powered his bike back toward the Ferrari for a second assault, Jesse leapt out of hiding and lashed out with his cane as if he were pinch-hitting with the bases loaded in the final game of the World Series. He clipped the rider across the face visor with enough force to shatter the plastic, but although the rider was stunned, he managed to maintain control of his bike. After narrowly avoiding collision with a cement pillar, he veered toward the exit and sped up the ramp to the street.

'Damn you, stop!' Jesse shouted as he hobbled after his attacker. He quickly realized it was a bootless quest, just as it was too late for him to get to his car and try to take up the chase. Frustrated, he tossed away the broken half of the cane still in his hand and limped to the elevator, then stopped off at his apartment long enough to change clothes. He contemplated calling the station about the attack but thought better of it. Hunger was still gnawing at him, and he decided to resume his weekly ritual of eating out at a nearby Japanese restaurant that offered the best sushi in the area as well as a big-screen television that was always tuned into the Monday Night ball game. After all he'd been through, he felt he deserved the diversion.

The restaurant was crowded, as usual, but as he picked his way through the throng, Jesse spotted one familiar face he hadn't expected to find here. Sandy McCoy was seated in a booth next to the sushi bar, nursing a small cup of saké as she nibbled from a bowl of crispy fried noodles. When she saw Jesse, she smiled slightly and waved him over.

'Small world, eh?' Jesse said as he slipped into the seat across from Sandy. 'Funny, I wouldn't have figured you for the sushi type.'

'Actually, I hate the stuff,' Sandy confessed. 'I came here to see you. Officer Farnsworth told me I might be able to find you here.'

'Voilà, you found me. What's up?'

Sandy took a deep breath. Coming here hadn't been an easy thing for her. 'I just thought it would be a good idea if we got to know each other a little better. It might help us to avoid any future misunderstandings at the office.'

'I see.' Jesse picked up a menu and glanced over the offerings as he nonchalantly asked, 'What did you have in mind?'

Sandy clasped her hands together and sat upright. 'This isn't a come-on, Jesse. How about just some good old-fashioned conversation?'

'Sounds fine to me, only I think we should order a little more saké to help loosen my tongue...'

One hour and two bottles of saké later, more than Jesse's tongue was loose. He was half-sprawled in his chair, laughing his way through a favourite anecdote that had to do with a prank he and Marty had pulled on Commander Altobelli for their superior's most recent birthday. Sandy was enjoying herself as well, and had even managed to sample part of the sushi platter Jesse had ordered for supper.

'I can't believe it... you actually brought this girl into Altobelli's office?'

Jesse nodded as he finished his latest dose of saké. 'Yeah, and it was one crazy scene, let me tell ya. There she was, stripping away as she sang "Happy Birthday" to him. Of course, by the time she finished the song, she turns out to be a he!'

'No!'

'Yes! Altobelli was so mad he busted the guy for impersonating a woman!'

They both broke out in a fresh fit of laughter. A waitress came by to see if they wanted more saké, but Jesse was ready for coffee. Sandy asked for tea. The mere suggestion of sobering up cut an edge through the gaiety they'd been sharing, and as the laughter died down, Sandy said, 'You really like the commander, don't you?'

Jesse shrugged his shoulders. 'We run hot and cold, if you know what I mean.'

'Sort of like us?'

'Yeah, sort of like us.' His coffee arrived and Jesse topped off the cup with cream. 'But maybe we've worked that out a little tonight, don't you think?'

'I hope so.'

'Sandy, are you sure there wasn't another reason you came by here tonight?'

Sandy stirred her tea, then took out the bag and set it near the edge of her saucer as she stared into her drink like a fortune teller seeking the future. 'That comment you made this morning . . . my not caring about the truth. It really bothered me.'

'It was a cheap shot,' Jesse apologized. 'I was upset. I'm sorry.'

'Well, I'm not so sure that I didn't deserve it.' Sandy added milk to her tea, then went on. 'Anyway, I spoke to the Commander and told him what you said about your friend's case. He thinks you're paranoid.'

'Hah!' Jesse grinned bitterly and shook his head. 'That's a good one. Tell me, Sandy, what do you think about all this?'

'I'm not sure,' she admitted. 'It's always been my job to paint a rosy picture about the department . . . it's just hard for me to accept that there could really be any corruption. But of course that's foolish. I mean, we're all only human, after all.'

'I can't believe Altobelli . . .'

'What, that he thinks you're being paranoid?'

Jesse looked Sandy in the eyes. 'You know why you were waiting so long for me to get here tonight? Somebody tried to kill me in the garage under my apartment, that's why. Does that sound like paranoia to you?'

TWENTY-FOUR

Commissioner Miller was at the podium in the City Council chambers, pitching a proposal for increased funds to be earmarked specifically for use in combating a recent and troubling increase in gang-related crime throughout Los Angeles, particularly in Commander Altobelli's jurisdiction. By way of visual aids to his presentation, he relied on a series of projected images flashed on a viewing screen behind him, depicting various police functions that would come into play should the City Council funnel the appropriate money into the operation – public awareness seminars; special SWAT training to deal with gang warfare; bilingual patrol teams to cruise crime-sensitive areas.

'And, to get to the bottom line in terms of impact,' Miller concluded, 'we project that the approval of funds for this task force will enable us to curtail all crimes traceable to gangs by a minimum of eighteen percent. On the merits of that statistic alone, I hope that we can count on your vote for a safer, saner Los Angeles. Thank you . . .'

There was a slight patter of applause from the gallery as the screen behind Commissioner Miller went blank and the chamber lights were turned back on in full force. The city's seven council persons were seated behind a long table that faced the gallery, and as Miller stepped down from the podium, their spokesman, Franklin Waters, leaned forward in his seat and spoke into the microphone mounted before him. 'Thank you, Commissioner Miller, for such a concise and, I think, convincing presentation. Rest assured that we intend to give the matter our highest priority. In fact, after a short adjournment, I suspect that we will vote on the matter during the course of new business. Now there will be a brief ten minute recess.'

As the Council filed out through a back door leading to their chambers, the citizens in the gallery broke out into whispers and low murmurs of conversation as they rose from their seats and either stretched or left the main room. Jesse had been running the slide projector during Miller's presentation, and as he began boxing the slide carousel, he overheard several people congratulating the Commissioner once more on his speech.

'A lot of the credit should be going to Miss McCoy,' Miller professed, nodding towards Sandy, who was standing next to Jesse. 'She's the one who compiled the slide show, which I like to call my "special effects".' He laughed lightly at his own joke, then turned back to address yet another well-wisher.

Commander Altobelli was there, too, and he wormed his way through the crowd to Jesse's side, where he asked, 'What's this I hear about somebody tying to kill you last night?'

'Word sure travels fast around here.' Jesse shot a quick glance at Sandy, who nodded demurely, then walked off to have a word with the head of a Chicano activism group that was volunteering its help in dealing with the scourge of gang violence in LA's barrios.

'You're running your own investigation, aren't you, Mach?' Altobelli charged. 'No sense pretending you aren't.'

Jesse finished closing the box holding the slides, then began dismantling the slide projector. Without looking at the Commander, he muttered, 'Gee, why should I have to run my own investigation with the thorough job IA's doing with it, hmmm?'

'Spare me your sarcasm, Mach, and listen to me.' Altobelli wagged his finger at Jesse as if it were a magic wand he hoped would impose a state of complete obedience on the young man. 'You're not a one-man police force, dammit! And the next time somebody tries to take you out, I want to hear about it.'

'Yeah yeah...' Jesse draped a plastic covering over the projector, then lifted it up and set it on the slide box.

'Understood, Mach?' Altobelli pressed. 'I want to hear about it!'

Commissioner Miller was standing within earshot of Jesse and Altobelli, and when he overheard about the attempt on Jesse's life, his face turned ashen and he quickly excused himself from the council chambers, claiming he had a pressing appointment to keep. The fact was, he had no appointment, and all the way out to Anthony Corrido's estate, he could only hope that the man would be there. Miller's heart was pounding like a raquetball against the walls of his chest by the time he pulled into the tree-lined driveway and waited for the gate to open for him. As much as he was enraged, Miller was also chilled with fear, and the combination had his adrenalin working overtime.

Corrido was working in his garage, dressed in a pair of denim overalls as he tinkered with a snowmobile he wanted to get back in top working condition before the first snowfall up in the mountains. He frowned at the sight of Miller's Mercedes pulling to a stop near the garage, and he walked over to greet the Commissioner without setting down the screwdriver he was using.

'Well, now, Commissioner, I figured you'd be calling me on the phone. You didn't need to drive all the way out here just to let me know about the next drop...'

'Forget about that,' Miller snapped. 'We had an agreement.'

'That's right. So what's the problem?'

'I'm talking about Mach! I said I'd handle him. Our agreement was there'd be no more murders! Let me tell you something, Corrido, if I –'

'Let's get one thing straight, right now!' Corrido interrupted, taking another step closer to Miller. 'You don't tell me anything. I tell you. Got it?'

Miller shook his head emphatically. 'No, sorry. Not any more. I'm out.'

'Out?'

'That's right!'

'I need that next shipment,' Corrido insisted. 'New York is expecting it. I'm not about to tell them I can't deliver. If you think I'm a rough customer, you ought to try crossing those boys some time . . .'

'I don't want to hear about it!' Miller turned around and headed back for his car, shouting over his shoulder, 'Tell them your source just dried up!'

Corrido looked over at his bodyguards and snapped his fingers. Like trained animals, they broke into brisk strides and intercepted Miller before he could get back into his car. When Corrido caught up with him, the Commissioner was pinned against the front end of his Mercedes. The side of his face was pressed against the hood.

'We have a business commitment and I expect you to live up to it, Miller.' Corrido set down the tip of his screwdriver and dragged it slowly across the hood of the Mercedes, scratching through four layers of metallic paint. He stopped when the tool was within a couple of inches of puncturing the Commissioner's cheek. 'Let me down, and I might just get carried away with your pretty little car and your pretty little face. You wouldn't like that, would you?'

Miller said nothing, but the fear in his eyes spoke volumes . . .

TWENTY-FIVE

Running on a treadmill was the last exercise of Jesse's fitness regime, and he was halfway through his required two miles when Norman dropped in to check on things. He was carrying a computer readout in one hand and a can of fruit juice in the other.

'Good news, Jesse,' he announced. 'I worked the bugs out of the hyperthrust mechanism! You know what that means, don't you?'

Jesse grinned as he continued to run. Between breaths, he said, 'Street Hawk's ready for the road, right?'

'That's what the readouts say,' Norman agreed, rattling the computer sheets. 'I can't believe it . . . after all these years of work, the time's finally come!'

'Congratulations, Norman.' Jesse stopped running and unhitched himself from the treadmill.

'Why did you stop?' Norman asked. 'You have another mile to go!'

'What's a mile among friends?'

'Are you sure it's not your leg?'

'Positive.' Jesse grabbed a towel and mopped his brow. 'Look, I just thought that maybe we ought to celebrate. You know, break the rules a little bit and have some fun. Drink something besides carrot juice, go have a look at some nice ladies in person instead of gawking at Jane on the wall over there. Let's party, Norman!'

Norman made a sour face and shook his head. 'I don't party, and I have no interest in damaging my brain cells with soaking them in alcohol, thank you.'

Jesse laughed as he wadded up his towel and threw it at

Norman. 'You need to loosen up, my friend. Join the human race.'

'I don't have time,' Norman declared. 'Look, now that Street Hawk's ready, I think we should start plotting a demonstration of its capabilities. I was considering these cocaine heists that have been plaguing the police department the past couple of months.'

'What about them?'

'You know the situation. Hijackers intercept a police transport van, disable it, then disappear without a trace. Why? Because the thieves are too fast for conventional means of pursuit. But not for Street Hawk...'

Jesse thought it over while he untied his shoelaces and pulled off his running shoes. 'Well, I'd like to get my hands on those guys as much as anyone, Norman. Especially when you figure one of them was probably the biker who tried to blow me away last night. Only problem is that I can't get the routes or departure schedules for the deliveries. There's no way I can ask around without the chief catching wind of it and giving me a good bust in the chops.'

'That's not a problem,' Norman replied. 'I can tie into the Coast Guard's computer and find out when they schedule a disposal.'

'Oh yeah?' After pulling off his socks, Jesse began massaging the soles of his aching feet. The more he heard about Norman's scheme, the more he liked it.

'We couldn't ask for a better situation,' Norman argued. 'Just think of it... two lightweight motorcycles out-manoeuvring both police cycles and squad cars. It's a natural for Street Hawk!'

Jesse stared past Norman and out of the plexiglass window at Street Hawk, which rested majestically on its platform in the main room of the command centre. 'Okay, Norman, I think we should go fot it.' With a wicked grin, he added, '... after I have a chance to take the bike on a test run.'

Norman downed the rest of his fruit juice, then tossed the can in the trash and told Jesse, 'All right, you've got yourself a deal!'

'Now you're talking!'

'Shower and suit up,' Norman said. 'By the time you're ready, I should have everything set up.'

With a manic howl of glee, Jesse headed for the shower. Norman left the exercise room and stared proudly at Street Hawk as he walked to the command module and started up the power. The bike was already linked to the computers, and when Norman inserted a specially-created floppy disk and punched up a set of commands, Street Hawk was automatically inspected, system by system, microchip by microchip, until the monitor screen lit up with a configuration that the motorcycle was indeed in perfect running condition.

In his own way, Jesse ran through his own mental checklist in preparation for his maiden ride on Street Hawk. It was all he could do to suppress the giddy, almost childlike joy he felt at the prospect of getting back on a bike for the first time since his disability. As he carefully donned his tight-fitting black racing suit, he recalled the hours of instruction Norman had drilled into him regarding the unique makeup of the superbike. More so than with any previous cycle he'd ever ridden, the utmost concentration would be required to ensure that he would return from the test ride intact. One didn't travel at speeds of up to three hundred miles an hour in a carefree state of mind. One mistake and they'd need tweezers and a spatula to clean him off the road.

Jesse's suit fitted him perfectly, and when he emerged into the main chamber, holding his helmet under his arm, he looked like a gladiator from the next century. He walked over to the command module, where Norman had cued up the vector map and was completing the last of his other preparations. Jesse informed him, 'I'm ready when you are, Norman... except for one thing. How do I get out of here...?'

TWENTY-SIX

There was a gigantic billboard attached to the side of the warehouse where Norman Tuttle based Operation Street Hawk, advertising a non-existent brand of soda water called Max. The billboard artwork depicted a bottle tilted in such a way that its cap faced out into the back alley, supposedly airbound due to a blast of effervescence from its tingling, refreshing contents. The reason why a massive billboard touting a fictional product faced an untravelled stretch of asphalt became instantly clear when the sign suddenly parted in the middle, creating an opening through which Jesse Mach launched himself into the air, riding the most highly sophisticated motorcycle ever to come off a drawing board.

Jesse brought the bike down gracefully and banked around the corner of the warehouse, grinning triumphantly behind his shielding visor. His knee had withstood the jolt of the landing, and as he guided Street Hawk through its gears, the smoothness of the ride gave him further reason for exultation. Whisking through the side streets of the city, testing the low-speed manoeuvrability of the cycle, he felt a joy that matched the euphoria of his first few rides on a dirt bike years ago.

'No problems?' Norman's voice soon buzzed in Jesse's ears.

'Nope,' Jesse confirmed. 'Works like a dream.'

'Good. Don't push it just yet, though. Take it out to the training area.'

'Will do.'

The 'training area' was a three mile section of highway currently closed off to the public for major repairs. Jesse reached it in less than ten minutes without encountering any possible snags in the bike's low-speed performance. After he had ridden between the barriers blocking off the highway, he reported back to Norman, 'I'm ready. How're the readouts at your end?'

'Everything checks out fine. I have to hand it to the selection committee, Jesse. You can break in a bike with finesse when you want to. I could have sworn you'd break the speed limit racing over here.'

'This isn't the first prototype I've been on,' Jesse reminded Norman. 'If there're going to be any problems, I like to be moving slow enough to keep the damage to a minimum.'

'Good for you. Now, though, I think we can start pushing ourselves.'

Jesse stopped the bike and stared straight ahead. Although it was a dark night, void of stars and lit by only a thin slice of moon, his visor illuminated his view of the highway, which lay before him like a deserted raceway. He could see several sawhorses spaced at regular intervals to indicate where the asphalt was in need of repair.

'Okay, Norman, what should I start with?'

'Series one . . . chase manoeuvres.'

Jesse gave the throttle a tentative rev to familiarize himself with the bike's distinctive drone. For years now, he'd developed a keen ear for judging a bike's RPMS just from the sound of the motor. Once he felt he had a bead on Street Hawk's mechanical purr, he let up on the throttle and patted the gas tank the way a jockey will stroke a thoroughbred before the big race.

'All right, sweetheart. Let's see what you can do.'

'Sweetheart?'

'I'm not talking to you, Norman.'

'I didn't think so. Proceed when you're ready.'

Jesse gave himself a silent countdown, then roared forward, building speed as he held his course on the highway median. As he was approaching the first sawhorse, he went into his first tight turn and Street Hawk handled the sudden change in direction flawlessly, dipping with the shift in weight and righting itself once Jesse had rounded the obstacle. By the time he had negotiated the fourth turn, Jesse was riding at the freeway speed limit. As he was approaching the end of the repair section, Jesse heard Norman confirming what he already knew.

'Beautiful, just beautiful. My monitors are picking up everything clearly. Street Hawk's outperforming all my expectations... and you're doing a fine job as well, Mach.'

'Thanks, Norman. Does that mean I get a star on my forehead when I get back?'

'No, but it does mean we can move into the second series. Just give me a second here to program it.'

As he waited, Jesse glanced down the length of roadway he'd just travelled, then said, 'Hey, Norman, at three hundred miles an hour, I'm gonna run out of track real quick.'

'I know. That's why I'm running a computer check on the freeway you link up with... there's minimal traffic and no patrol cars out, so you can go ahead and run past the barriers. Just be careful.'

'I plan to, Norman.'

'Okay, you're cleared. Remember, hyperthrust is computer assist. All you have to do is hold on and make sure you stay on the road.'

'That's all? Gee, what a cakewalk...'

'No more jokes, Mach. Concentrate. Pick up your speed and brace yourself. I'll flash your visor readout when you're down to ten seconds.'

Jesse took in a deep breath, then started off, opening up the throttle.

'Ten... nine... eight...' he whispered as the countdown ticked off on his visor. 'Seven... six... five...'

The highway was turning into a blur. Jesse was already travelling over a hundred and twenty miles an hour in half the time it would have taken him on a more conventional bike.

'Four... three... two...'

A rear seat support snapped up into position behind Jesse to keep the force of hyperthrust from pulling him off the bike. The digital readout on his visor told him he was up to one hundred and seventy miles an hour now.

'One... *zerooo!*'

Jesse could feel the sudden lunge of the bike as Norman

activated the hyperthrust mode. To his amazement, though, the bike held smoothly to the road and he felt little wind resistance despite the incredible speed he was travelling at. Two hundred and fifty... two hundred and sixty... seventy... eighty...

'Three hundred!'

Jesse was out on the open freeway now, staying in the fast lane to avoid the other vehicles on the road, which seemed to be crawling in comparison to his clip.

'Slow it down!' Norman's voice suddenly buzzed in Jesse's helmet. 'You're going to overheat it if you don't watch it!'

'But I'm not doing anything, Norman! You're the one with a finger on the gas pedal...'

'You've got the throttle open still and that overrides me. Ease off!'

Jesse realized that he had indeed left his wrist instinctively twisted to hold the throttle wide open. He let up on it and immediately Street Hawk began to decelerate at a programmed rate that allowed him to maintain full control over the brake and steering controls. By the time the bike was cruising at the speed limit, he was closer to the city and traffic was getting thicker.

'What a rush that was, Norman!'

'I'll bet it was. That's enough for tonight, though. Bring her in.'

'Now?' Jesse grumbled. 'I was just starting to have some fun. Come on, Norman, the night is still young.'

'Mach. Boogie your butt back home. Do you read me?'

Jesse veered over two lanes and took the next exit shooting off from the freeway. 'Okay, chief,' he said drearily. 'But after being off a bike for so long, you're really being heartless by dragging me in, Norman.'

'That's life in the big city, Jesse...'

TWENTY-SEVEN

Another aspect of life in the big city was robbery, and when Jesse left the freeway to head back to the warehouse, he found himself approaching the scene of a liquor store hold-up. A pair of vicious-looking hoods burst out of the corner market and dashed toward an old battered Chevy idling at the kerb. One of the thugs was clutching a bag filled with the liquor store's receipts; the other was armed with a sawn-off shotgun, which he promptly levelled at the doors. With a loud roar, a charge of buckshot smashed the door's glass and sent the proprietor diving to the linoleum for cover.

'Let's make tracks!' the gunman shouted as he climbed into the car and slammed the door shut.

From his vantage point back at the command module, Norman witnessed Jesse's approach to the robbery scene over Street Hawk's monitor screen. He didn't like what he was seeing.

'Mach, what are you doing?'

'I think we're going to have to test our series three operations,' Jesse replied.

'You are not cleared for encounter,' Norman asserted. 'Repeat . . . you are not cleared for encounter!'

'Too late,' Jesse said, stopping his bike directly in the path of the Chevy. 'I'm already here.'

The driver of the getaway car slammed on the brakes and his cohorts gaped at the obstacle preventing their escape.

'What's that?' the man with the money wanted to know.

The gunman fed a fresh cartridge into his shotgun, then rolled down his window and leaned out, chortling, 'It's gonna be dead meat when I get through with it!'

The blast from the shotgun chewed up the asphalt in front of Street Hawk but was too far off the mark to cause any damage. Jesse held his ground as he activated the weapon turret between his handlebars and locked aim on the Chevy by way of the monocle targeting system in his helmet.

'This better work, Norman, or else you're going to have a slight mess on your hands.'

After adjusting the strength of the bikegun's output, Jesse unleashed a particle beam that crackled forward like a trained bolt of blue lightning, engulfing the Chevy and shaking it as if it weighed no more than a tumbleweed caught up in a crosswind. From within the ominous-looking force field, shrieks of terror sounded above the rumbling of the car's tortured engine.

'Had enough, boys?' Jesse cut the power and the particle beam instantly vanished from view. The Chevy settled on the pavement, smoke spewing from beneath the hood. The driver was unable to get the engine started, and the two men beside him were too frightened to leave the vehicle or risk Street Hawk's wrath by firing at Jesse again.

'Hey, Norman, that's a nifty little popgun you outfitted this bike with. Did you see me rattle that Chevy?'

'Yes, I did,' Norman said. 'I hope you realize that if you had set the beam a fraction higher, you would have blown up the car, not to mention yourself, the bike, and half the block!'

'Give me a little credit, Norman. I've watched enough "Star Trek" re-runs to know the difference between a phaser setting for stun and for kill...'

During Jesse's standoff with the robbers, the liquor store owner had managed to put a call through to the police, and soon the night air was alive with the sound of sirens.

'Mach, what are you waiting for, a commendation?' Norman pestered in Jesse's ear. 'Get out of there!'

Jesse waited until the proprietor was charging out of his store with a shotgun of his own before he started to ride off. By then, however, the first of the squad cars screeched into view, skidding to a sideways stop that effectively blocked the road. Within a matter of seconds, another cruiser arrived, further hemming Jesse in. Officers poured out of the vehicles and, mistaking Jesse for an accomplice, took aim at him and shouted for him to surrender.

'Sorry, Norman...'

'Sorry nothing, Mach! Get out of there! It's too soon for us to tip our hand!'

'Well, you see, there's this slight problem,' Jesse said. 'I don't think this bike's equipped to ride through things, especially bullet showers and police barricades...'

'Then go *over* them!' Norman said. 'Use your vertical lift, dammit!'

'My vertical lift!' Jesse felt like Aladdin on the day he learned about the powers of his lamp. 'Of course.'

'Get off that bike and throw your hands up!' one of the officers shouted at Jesse. Jesse recognized the man as Mike Holt and was grateful that his visor hid his features from view. He wasn't ready to try to explain things, not just yet.

'Here goes...' Jesse powered Street Hawk forward, building as much speed as was possible in so short a space, then triggered the vertical lift. A volley of gunfire raced beneath the bike as it vaulted upward and over the patrol cars, startling the officers into a state of profound shock. Making a perfect two-point landing, Jesse opened the throttle and veered around yet another cruiser, which tried to give chase for a couple of blocks before falling hopelessly behind the speeding cycle.

'Any other tests you want me to try, Norman?'

'Don't be glib with me, Mach! You came so close to screwing up it isn't funny! Now get that bike back here before I override your functions and bring it back here by myself!'

'Can you really do that, Norman?'

'Try me!'

Jesse shook his head and made a right turn that brought him back into the warehouse district. 'No thanks, Norman. I'm coming in. Fire up the landing lights...'

TWENTY-EIGHT

By nine o'clock the following morning, the police station was besieged by members of the press, who were directed to a cramped conference room and told to wait until the Commander was free to speak with them. Rumours had been flying since late the previous evening, and when Altobelli finally entered the chamber and eyed the reporters, he knew he was going to have trouble blunting the wave of speculation surrounding the bizarre turn of events that had taken place outside the liquor store. The questions started filling the air even before he reached the podium, and the Commander scowled at the flashing bulbs of press photographers, saying nothing until some semblance of order had come to the room.

'First of all,' he began, speaking in the bland monotone he always saved for the announcement of sensational news, 'I'm sure you'll all be happy to hear that we now have in custody the three men responsible for the series of corner store robberies that have plagued our division for much of the past four weeks...'

'Come on, Commander!' one of the reporters blurted out. 'We know all about that. What about the masked man on the motorcycle?'

'Yeah!' another man shouted. 'Is it true that there was – ?'

'If I don't have it quiet, this news conference is over!' Altobelli shouted. As he waited for the furore to die down again, the Commander spotted Sandy and Jesse standing near the doorway. Jesse was holding an armload of pamphlets and Sandy had a clipboard. She made a gesture, inquiring if Altobelli wanted her help in handling the reporters. He nodded gratefully, and as she threaded her way through the press, he continued, 'Officer Mach from our Public Relations department has a handout for you with more pertinent information on the arrest and the alleged perpetrators. With that in mind, I'll touch briefly on a second item... Yes, an unidentified man riding a custom motorcycle was also reported at the robbery scene. When he was approached for questioning, however, he fled.'

'You mean he flew!'

The wisecrack triggered an undercurrent of chuckles and murmurs amongst the press. A female reporter rose on her tiptoes and raised her voice to be heard above the din.

'The owner of the market said the motorcycle rider stopped the robbers from fleeing by shooting some sort of ray gun at the getaway car...'

'No comment,' Altobelli snapped.

'Would the robbers be in custody today if the masked marauder hadn't shown up?'

'Yes!'

'Would you consider him a hero?' another reporter asked.

Altobelli shot Sandy an exasperated glance as she joined him at the podium. He told the press, 'Look, as far as the Police Department is concerned this rider is operating outside the jurisdiction of the law. He's not a hero – he's a vigilante, and we have no intention of turning the city into something out of a bad Charles Bronson movie. My orders are to see that this man is apprehended before he ends up hurting someone. Now, thank you, that's all I have to say...'

'How long before you expect to catch him, Commander?'

As Altobelli fled the press, escaping out of the back door, Sandy stepped forward to the podium and offered an officious smile. 'Thank you for your questions. As the Commander said, you can pick up more details on the arrests as you're leaving. If and when there are any new developments, you'll be kept posted...'

'Yeah, sure...'

There was a steady stream of grumbling as the reporters filed out of the conference room, snapping up the press packets Jesse was handing out. He could sense their collective scepticism about the limited information Altobelli had divulged about the mysterious interloper who had thwarted the robbers. He struggled to keep an impassive expression on his face as he listened to the various wild guesses being made as to the rider's identity. If they only knew that they were looking right at him...

'Hey, Jesse,' Freddie Williams called out as he fought the human current in the hallway and made his way to Jesse's side. 'Bernie from the lab just stopped by, looking for you. He said he's got something you're looking for. I can finish this for you if you want to check it out.'

'Oh yeah?' Jesse handed the rest of the flyers to Freddie, then gave him a pat on the back. 'You're a gentleman and a scholar!'

Freddie blushed at the compliment. 'Well, I try...'

When Jesse tracked down Bernie in the lab, he found the technician labouring over a beaker of cloudy fluid that bubbled above the open flame of a bunsen burner.

'Freddie told me you had something...'

Bernie nodded as he finished stirring the concoction in the beaker. Going over to his cluttered desk, he snatched up a computer printout. 'I gave it the full treatment. Solubility, pyrolysis gas chromatograph, and infra-red spectro photometer.'

'Uh, Bernie, you lost me, I'm afraid.'

'Never mind that.' Bernie pried free the small plastic bag taped to the sheet and handed it to Jesse. The bag contained the black paint chips. 'What you have here is a carbon pigment base, five layers of clear metallic lacquer – pearl flakes, not aluminium. Around ten coats... good quality... and very expensive.'

Jesse pocketed the bag. 'So, I'm looking for a custom paint shop, right?'

'That's your job,' Bernie said, going back to the beaker and stirring its contents once more. 'I just figure out what it is, not where it comes from... although I would tend to agree that a paint shop might be your best bet.'

'Thanks, Bernie. Sherlock Holmes has nothing on you...'

'Good luck, Jesse.' Bernie dipped a spoon into the mixture he was boiling, then sampled it. Smacking his lips, he decided, 'Needs more salt.'

On the way back to his office, Jesse made a stop to pick up all the various yellow page directories for Los Angeles and outlying counties. It was a hefty load, and by the time he'd carried it to his desk, his arms were aching. Sitting down, he was just beginning to flip through the pages of the nearest directory when Sandy came in.

'Freddie told me you were onto something.'

'Sort of.'

Sandy watched Jesse scan the yellow pages. 'Is it evidence of some sort?'

'Just a lead.' Jesse reached for the plastic bag and handed it to Sandy. 'It's paint from the truck that killed Marty. I had the lab break it down. I.A. should have run it through a long time ago.'

'Have you told any of this to Altobelli?'

'What for?'

'Maybe he can open things up and see what's going on.'

'Or maybe it'd just end up lost in the shuffle. I'm not taking that chance. My mother had this saying – if you want something done right, do it yourself.' As he tracked down the section in the directory he was looking for, Jesse moaned, 'Oh, this is great! There're three pages of custom paint shops just in this book alone!'

Sandy sat down across from Jesse and picked up another of the directories, explaining, 'Thomas Jefferson also had a saying. I forget the actual wording, but it was something to the effect that a person has to know when to delegate responsibilities in the name of greater efficiency.'

'You're offering to help me?' Jesse said. 'I don't believe it!'

Sandy smiled slyly. 'Let's just say my reporter's instincts have been perked up . . .'

TWENTY-NINE

The Classic Craft Body Shop looked like the best prospect, because it was the place located closest to the desert where the black pickup had run both Jesse and Marty off the cliff. Sandy had agreed to check on the paint shops outside the city limits, and so it was she who pulled into the lot at Classic Craft. The shop was located in an industrial building made of cinder block and steel. It shared space with a dozen other small businesses, most of which dealt with various aspects of automobile repair and refurbishing. After checking at the main desk, Sandy was sent back to the work area, where a pot-bellied welder was applying the heat of his acetylene torch to the front fender of a partially-restored '57 Thunderbird. It was nearly a minute and a half after Sandy had gotten the man's attention before he finally stopped what he was doing and raised his welding helmet. The man's pudgy features were centred around the stub of a half-smoked cigar. He paused to light it with the torch before blowing smoke Sandy's way and asking, 'Yeah? What's yer problem?'

Jesse had given Sandy half of the paint chips, and she held out the clear Baggie containing them. 'I was just wondering if you might be able to remember having done a paint job in this colour.'

The welder squinted at the bag, then sneered at Sandy, 'You gotta be kidding!! How the hell should I know from lookin' at those?'

Sandy calmly rattled off the technical description of the chips that she'd memorized from Bernie's computer analysis, then added, 'You must know if you even *do* that kind of work.

I mean, a job that thorough you'd have to remember doing, right?'

The man's sneer turned into something more lascivious and he chuckled, 'You done yer homework, haven't you, little lady?'

Sandy took a step back from the man and stiffened. 'Look, can you help me or can't you?'

'That all depends,' the man cackled. 'What's in it fer me if I *do* help ya?'

Before Sandy could respond to the welder's come-on, another man emerged from the storage room, wearing an apron splotched with a dozen different colours of paint.

'What's goin' on here, Zeke?' he asked the welder.

Sandy turned to the second man and said, 'I was looking for some information about a custom paint job on a black pickup truck.'

'Well, Zeke wouldn't know about that,' the man in the apron said. 'Hell's bells, the only thing he can paint is the town, right, Zeke?'

Zeke made a face at his partner and stubbed out his cigar before lowering the hood of his welding mask and going back to work. Sandy showed her paint samples to the other man and explained the information she was seeking.

'Sorry, but the only paint job I've done that comes close to that's a number I did on an old Ferrari a few months back, and that was in red.'

Sandy took the bag back and slipped it in her purse. 'Well, thanks for taking a look, anyway.'

'My pleasure. If it's any consolation, you're right about that being a rare type of paint job. If I were you, I'd call around to a few places and see if I could jar somebody's memory. Apt to be less wear and tear on you in the long run.'

'I might just do that.'

Sandy carefully avoided Zeke on her way out, then got in her car and drove to a post office she'd passed on the way to Custom Craft. Inside the building, she found a phone she could operate with her calling card instead of with an endless supply of dimes. Setting the yellow pages on the counter next to the phone, she started calling other paint shops in the area.

Between Aames Auto Detailing and Zenith Precision Painters she had more than twenty calls to make...

Jesse was making the rounds in his Mustang, and he'd already made stops at two shops without getting the information he was looking for. Now he was in Hollywood, checking out a back-alley operation called Star's Delight Chrome and Custom Works. Three long-haired bikers in denim vests and worn jeans were collaborating on the transformation of a once modest-looking '84 Cougar into a garish chartreuse eyesore with airbrushed dice painted in a repeating pattern around the entire frame.

'Uh, nice work, guys,' Jesse remarked as he got out of his car and watched the bikers at work.

The tallest of the other men sniggered as he stood back and looked the car over. 'Ugly as sin, isn't it? They're gonna use it in some new TV show about some Vegas crooner dude who works for the CIA when he goes on tours overseas.'

'Sounds like a real winner,' Jessie said.

'Yeah, tell me about it. But, what the heck, as long as they shell out cash on the barrelhead, we'll paint 'em naked dancing girls on the hoods of limousines.'

Jesse laughed along with the man's joke as he got out his paint samples. 'I was wondering if you could take a look at these and tell me if it looks like something that might come off a paint job of yours.'

The tall man's eyes narrowed suspiciously and he scratched at his Fu Manchu moustache as he gave Jesse a quick once-over. 'You a cop, man? We don't like cops.'

'Not even bike cops?' Jesse nodded in the direction of three chopped Harleys parked in the corner of the parking lot. 'Unless I miss my guess, those are old Highway Patrol hogs you guys picked up in auction. Seems like we should have more in common than not. Besides, I'm not after you. I want the guy whose black pickup these chips belong to.'

'How'd you know about those Harleys, man?'

'I love bikes, that's all.'

Having established a camaraderie, Jesse held out the paint chips again. This time the tall man took the bag and peered in at its contents. He quickly shook his head, though, and gave the samples back. 'Sorry, man. I haven't used pearl flakes in years. Too damn expensive.'

'Know anybody around these parts that might?'

The tall man thought it over then gave Jesse the names of a couple of other shops he might check. Jesse thanked the man and headed back to his car. Before he could get in, a portable beeper in his shirt pocket started sounding off.

'Good timing, Norman,' Jesse muttered as he turned off the beeper and started up his engine. As he was pulling out of the driveway, the tall man waved to get his attention.

'You ever thought of slappin' some flames on the sides of that Mustang? We could cut a nice deal with you.'

'I'll keep that in mind,' Jesse said. He crossed the shop's ad off in the yellow pages, then shifted gears and drove off planning to stop at another shop or two on the way to see what Norman was trying to get in touch with him about.

Sandy plopped onto a stool near the counter at the Bazilian Brothers Paint and Custom Shop. Pio Bazilian had just slipped into the back room with the paint samples to consult with his brother. This was the third place Sandy was following up on after having confirmed over the phone that they did the sort of paint job she was concerned about. Her hopes for success were beginning to sag, and she wasn't looking forward to the five other stops she had promised herself she would make before calling it a day.

When the doors of the back room swung inward, it was Dom Bazilian who entered. He was an anaemically thin man in his early seventies, but there was a sparkle of life in his eyes and he spoke with the vitality of a man half his age as he dangled the Baggie and told Sandy, 'It's ours.'

'It is?' Sandy was dumbfounded. 'Are you sure?'

'Sure am. Recognize it anywhere.' Dom set the paint chips on the counter. 'It was this big black truck . . . pickup with balloon-type tyres. Ten coats the guy wanted. Pearl metallic. Cost a fortune, but it sure came out a beaut . . .'

Sandy could barely contain her excitement. She slipped from the stool and leaned across the counter, asking Dom,

'Would you happen to have a record of that job?'

Dom ran his spindly fingers through the thin strands of his sparse hair and shook his head. 'No. We aren't big on keepin' books. I just remember the man paid us in cash. Brand new hundred dollar bills, as a matter of fact. I gave one of 'em to my grandson for his graduation. Say, you aren't from the IRS, are you?'

'Oh, heavens no...' Sandy glanced down at a pile of magazines on the counter. The title of one of them jumped out at her and she used it. 'I work for *Auto Craft* magazine.'

'Oh yeah? Maybe you can do a story on us, huh?'

Sandy decided to milk her charade for all it was worth. Smiling suggestively, she told the thin man, 'Well, I think I might be able to do that, provided I can track down this gentleman in the black pickup. You know, for pictures.'

'That'd be fine, real fine!' Dom snapped his fingers and pointed out the back window at the parking lot behind the shop. 'As luck would have it, the man who owns that Mercedes knows the guy with the truck.'

Sandy glanced out and spotted the silver 208SE parked along a dividing wall. 'I could swear I've seen that car somewhere before...'

'It had a long, ugly scratch across the hood,' Dom told her. 'He didn't want to talk about it. Just wanted it fixed quick. As a matter of fact, he should be by to pick it up after lunch, if you'd like to wait.'

'Do you have his name?'

Dom shook his head. 'He pays cash, too.'

'Thanks, maybe I'll wait for him. Listen, do you mind if I go have a look at the job you did on his hood? My boss has some scratches on his Chrysler that he's been looking to have painted over. Maybe I can throw a little business your way.'

'Be my guest.' Another customer had just entered the shop, so Dom pointed to the side door and Sandy let herself out. She walked over to the Mercedes, still feeling a tinge of familiarity with the vehicle. She circled around the car, admiring the paint job which had totally covered the scratch on the hood, then gave into temptation and tried the front door. It wasn't locked, and she nonchalantly opened it. After looking around to make sure no one was watching, she stooped down and leaned inside the car, where she began rummaging through the glove compartment to find some identification. At the bottom of a heap of maps, notepads, brochures, and other paraphernalia, she was finally able to get her hands on the vehicle's registration papers. The name printed on the registration was that of one Thomas Miller, and lest there be any doubt in her mind as to which Thomas Miller that might be, when she closed the glove compartment and backed out of the car, she found herself facing none other than the Police Commissioner, who was discreetly aiming a .22 calibre handgun at her midsection.

'I understand you're looking for a friend of mine, Ms McCoy,' he said, menace lurking beneath the calm in his voice.

THIRTY

Norman was going out of his mind with impatience. He'd already prepared Street Hawk for the road and double-checked all functions on the command module to make sure they were operational, and still Jesse hadn't shown up or so much as responded to his call. He was about to page Jesse again when the door to the lab opened. Norman slammed down the phone and turned on Jesse, howling, 'Where have you been, Mach?!'

'Hey, lighten up, Norman!' After failing to come up with any sure leads as a result of his day's work, Jesse was in no mood for Norman's agitation. 'I know this may surprise you, but I have a life of my own once I leave this place. I don't sit around twiddling my thumbs waiting for your blessed bleeper to go off!'

'I know that, but this is a priority matter,' Norman declared. 'Suit up. You're going out.'

'Out? What's up?'

'I picked up a transmission from the Coast Guard a couple of hours ago. There's a drug disposal scheduled for this afternoon.'

Jesse slowly began to take off his coat and tie. 'Seems like awfully short notice.'

'Apparently it only came up this morning, so it was a surprise to them, too. They probably were hoping that if they did it without warning, there wouldn't be much time for the bike thieves to make a move. I have a feeling that won't be the case though.' Norman saw Jesse dawdling and raised his voice again. 'Will you hurry up and change! The van's probably on the street right now!'

'Okay, okay!' Jesse kicked off his shoes and padded into the exercise room, where his racing suit was waiting for him in one of the lockers. As he put the outfit on, he asked Norman, 'You didn't happen to catch wind of the van's travel route to the harbour, did you? Or am I supposed to –'

'I'm working on it, Mach!' Norman cued up the vector map and activated several radio scanners. 'I'm monitoring police frequency. If there's a hit, we'll know about it . . . and if you get your butt in gear, you might even be close enough to the action to do something about it!'

'I read you, Norman, loud and clear.' Jesse zipped himself into the racing suit, then fastened his riding boots and advanced toward Street Hawk.

As he handed Jess his helmet, Norman said, 'I managed to alter the hyperthrust program so that if you forget to take your hand off the throttle it won't matter.'

'You don't know how good that makes me feel,' Jesse sighed as he straddled the bike and carefully adjusted his helmet so that it fitted properly. 'Okay, I'm ready when you are. Just for the record, though, am I supposed to stick around if I save the day again?'

'No, you're to report back here immediately. I'll break the news on my own terms when I think the time is right.'

'Whatever you say, Norman. Maybe I should just leave a silver bullet and let 'em think I'm the great grandson of the Lone Ranger . . .'

As an added precaution against potential robbery, the police van carrying the most recent load of confiscated cocaine was being accompanied by a squad car and five additional officers on its cross-city journey to San Pedro. The cargo was twice the size of the previous shipment, another reason for the increased security. However, none of these measures was sufficient enough once Commissioner Miller leaked the particulars about the delivery to Anthony Corrido. When the two police vehicles were proceeding down a sparsely travelled section of Sepulveda Boulevard near Manchester, a little less than halfway to their destination, Corrido was waiting for them.

'Right on time,' he said to himself as he glanced at the dashboard clock in his black pickup. Rather than giving chase this time, Corrido had opted for a less indirect way of making a hit. He was parked up on an overpass that gave him a clear view of the roadway below. When he saw the patrol car coming up on a carefully marked section of the road, Corrido grasped a remote detonator and gave the plunger a firm shove with the butt of his palm.

An explosive charge had been attached to the underside of a manhole cover in the middle of Sepulveda Boulevard. When it was detonated, the charge sent the heavy lid bursting upward into the underside of the patrol car, which had been travelling over it at the time of the explosion. The concussive force of the booby-trap was powerful enough to flip the cruiser as if it were no more than a flapjack on a hot grill. Before the driver of the van could effectively react, the two police vehicles collided in a crunch of metal that left half the officers unconscious and the other men so stunned they were easy game for the two cyclists who soon roared onto the scene of the accident, wearing gas masks beneath their helmets as they tossed canisters of tear gas into both the van and the up-ended patrol car.

'Good show,' Corrido whispered smugly as he stared down at the results of his handiwork.

Norman was riding the crest of his own emotional current. Riveted to the chair before his command module, he was simultaneously tracing Street Hawk's position on the vector map, viewing Jesse's perspective of the city streets he was riding through, and keeping an eye on a computer printer that was linked up to his radio scanners and other surveillance equipment.

'Still nothing, Mach,' Norman reported, 'But I have a hunch you should cut more westward before you go any further south.'

'If you say so, Norman, but I'll bet you a quarter I'm on the right track going this way.'

'I never gamble.'

'What do you do for fun, Norman? Look at computer

magazines with software centrefolds?'

'I get all the gratification I need from my work. And besides... wait a second, I've got something.' Norman turned to the computer printer, which was spelling out the location where the police van had just been reported as down. 'You're lucky you didn't bet me, Mach. It's going down at Manchester and Sepulveda. I'm locking in the coordinates.'

'Going to give me a little push, is that it?'

'That's right. There's a drainage channel two blocks south of you. Get down in it and I'll be able to take you up to hyperthrust. With any luck, you'll catch those thieves with their hands in the till...'

Jesse quickly left the main street he was riding along and took an alley the two blocks to the drainage channel, one of many such conduits that ran through the city, carrying runoff water from rainstorms to the coast. The area was fenced off, but with the help of his vertical lift, Jesse was able to clear the barbed wire and land squarely on the upper edge of the channel. After guiding Street Hawk down the steep incline of the concrete embankment, he was riding along the level base of the channel, which was roughly half the size of a regular traffic lane.

'We're ready when you are, Norman.'

'Countdown,' Norman told him, activating the hyperthrust system back at the warehouse. 'Six seconds... five... four... three... two... one...'

Jesse clenched his teeth and held on tightly as he felt the drab grey of the concrete blurred on either side of him, and he could barely make out the passing outline of buildings and trees that filled out the uppermost edges of his view through the cineramic visor.

'I have no idea where I am, Norman, so you're going to have to let me know when I'm supposed to bail out...'

'Don't worry, I will. Just make sure you hold your position and don't wander into the runoff...'

Norman was speaking about the lowest section of the drainage channel, just a few feet away from where Jesse was riding. There the concrete was slick with algae and occasional puddles of water. If Jesse were to dip down into that area, the odds were that the bike would immediately hydroplane out of control, and with nothing but hard cement to cushion any falls, his chances of surviving such a *faux pas* were negligible.

It took Jesse less than five minutes to cover a stretch of the city that would have easily taken half an hour if he'd been restricted to following surface streets and keeping well within the speed limit. Norman prompted him when he was coming up on the intersection of Sepulveda and Manchester, and when he came out of hyperthrust and banked up the side of the embankment, Jesse relied on vertical lift to get him back over the fence and onto a side street.

'Okay, take a quick right, then two lefts and you're there!' Norman told him. 'From what I can gather, no police are there yet . . .'

Jesse leaned with the first turn, tilting Street Hawk sharply to compensate for the speed at which he was travelling. Once he was sure there was no other traffic to contend with, he opened the throttle even more on the next two turns, almost dragging his leg across the asphalt from the angle the bike took. With one final burst of speed, he came upon the two disabled police vehicles, which were interlocked like automotive wrestlers fighting a standstill battle. A handful of unconscious police officers lay near the car and van, and the two masked cyclists were just boarding their dirt bikes. From the make of the bikes and the outfits the riders were wearing, Jesse knew at once that one of them was the biker who had tried to kill him at his apartment complex. As he was about to give chase, Jesse spotted something out of the corner of his eye and suddenly froze in place. Up on the overpass, he saw Corrido's black pickup. The mere sight of the truck was enough to trigger an almost overpowering flash of *déjà vu.* For a moment, Jesse recalled in vivid detail the events immediately preceding the collision that had almost cost him his life.

'Mach, what the hell are you doing!' Norman's voice screeched in his ear. 'Intercept! Do you copy? *Intercept*!'

Jesse snapped out of his momentary trance. To his dismay, Corrido's truck had vanished from the overpass. The two cyclists were racing northward on Sepulveda, but traffic was too busy and they quickly took left turns, with Jesse in close pursuit. Street Hawk was almost sideswiped when Jesse raced to beat a changing traffic signal, but he managed to execute the turn and leave Sepulveda behind as the first of several police squad cars were converging on the area.

The cocaine thieves fled through a quiet suburban neighbourhood, causing several accidents as they cut corners and sped across lawns in an attempt to gain some distance on Jesse, who determinedly stayed on their track, closing the gap between them, yard by yard.

When they came upon the campus of Loytola Marymount University, the two bikers left the streets altogether and rode onto the college grounds, digging up the manicured lawn and sending students diving out of their way as they sped by. Although this manoeuvre gained them a few seconds, Jesse didn't lose them, since he only had to take a quick glance before him to pick up the route of chaos and destruction that cut through the heart of the campus.

'Be careful, Mach!'

'Sure thing, Mom,' Jesse said as he veered to avoid a water fountain. Ahead, he spotted the thieves rising up a steep-pitched slope leading to a cluster of large buildings. There was a pedestrian walkway that spanned the same incline, and Jesse took advantage of his vertical lift to leap up to the bridge.

'Nice jump, Jesse, but you have to watch those landings.'

'Norman, I'm in the middle of a high speed chase, for cryin' out loud. This is no time for lectures about finesse!'

'Well, there's always room for improvement.'

'Gee, maybe you can write that out on a poster and I'll put it over my bed.'

'I don't see them on the monitor any more, Mach. Did you lose . . . never mind, there they are . . .'

The bikers were leaving the campus now and resuming their flight down a narrow side street. Jesse picked up his speed and thought he was on the verge of overtaking the others when a young boy on a bicycle suddenly rode out in front of him. Jesse instinctively slammed on his brakes and tightened his grip on the handlebars, skidding sharply to one side to avoid hitting the youth or either of the parked cars from between which he'd appeared.

The boy on the bicycle stared fearfully at Jesse, then quickly pedalled off, pumping his legs for all they were worth. Jesse glared at the youth for a moment, then righted Street Hawk and hurried to the corner he'd seen the cyclists take. To his surprise, he found that the roadway ended abruptly after a few dozen yards. Concrete walls rose up a good twelve feet on either side of the dead end, making it impossible for the bikers to have scaled them without a vertical jump capability rivalling that of Street Hawk.

'I lost them,' Jesse moaned forlornly. 'After all that, I lost them . . .'

THIRTY-ONE

The windows of Commissioner Miller's Mercedes were darkly tinted to ensure anonymity while he was driving, and now he found them more useful than ever. They allowed him to blindfold Sandy so she couldn't see where he was taking her as he left the city. The roads leading to Anthony Corrido's desert mansion were relatively free of traffic, too, so Miller was able to handle driving with only one hand on the wheel. He kept his gun trained on Sandy with the other. Sandy was terrified, but refused to show it. Forcing herself to remain calm, she strained her ears in the hopes of hearing certain telltale sounds that might help her guess where she was being taken.

'You shouldn't have let Mach talk you into playing detective with him, Ms McCoy,' Miller said as he drove past the recreation area where Marty and Jesse had come with their bikes prior to the calamity that had triggered the events leading to Sandy's predicament. Even though Miller had the car windows rolled up and was playing music to further mask the many outside sounds, Sandy was able to hear the collective drone of off-road vehicles.

'As long as we're lecturing, Commissioner,' she said, 'you shouldn't have gotten yourself involved with whoever it is that's responsible for Marty Walsh's murder. Look at you. You're racking up federal offences . . . kidnapping, assault with a deadly weapon –'

'I don't need you to tell me the law!' Miller shouted. There was a tremble in his voice, and Sandy realized that the man was every bit as frightened as she was. She rode silently for the next few miles, concentrating on the nervousness she could sense coming from the Commissioner.

'Something tells me you're not in this thing willingly,' she finally said. 'What do they have on you?'

'Please be quiet, Ms McCoy. Don't make this any more difficult than it has to be.'

But Sandy pressed on, 'I've known you for two years, Commissioner. I saw that you were under a lot of stress the past few months, but I didn't guess why. You got in over your head with somebody, didn't you? You hadn't figured that people were going to end up being killed, or that –'

'That's enough, Ms McCoy!'

'Look, why don't you put a stop to it, right now! Cut your losses while you still can. If you put a finger on a cop killer, you know that it'll look good for you. As Commissioner, you can cover yourself... say you were over-zealous and thought you'd try to work your own undercover operation...'

Miller laughed bitterly. 'What kind of a sublime idiot do you take me for, anyway? Nobody in their right mind would believe a crock like that –'

'Then just blow the whistle and deny anything the criminals might charge you with! It would be just their word against yours.'

'It's more than words, dammit!' Miller blurted out. 'They have evidence that would put me away! Now will you shut up? I'm in this too deep to turn back, so don't try softening me up. I don't want to have to hurt you, but if you force my hand I'll have no choice!'

Miller pulled off the highway and headed down the main road leading to Corrido's mansion. His brow was beaded with perspiration, and his hands were clammy on the wheel. What if he were to drive on, he wondered. Maybe the woman had a point. He still had a flawless reputation. If he could buy some time and think of a way of wrangling the evidence Corrido was holding on him, he might be able to emerge from this whole dreary mess unscathed. As he thought about it, the idea gained more credence, but he decided it'd be better for him to act quickly instead of stalling for time. Things were happening too fast now, especially with another cocaine heist going down today. If things screwed up on that front and

Corrido was apprehended, it would be too late for him to save himself. No, he had to get to the mansion and somehow find the documents that the other man was holding . . . documents which implicated Miller with taking bribes from organized crime and using his influence to get several arrested mob leaders out of jail on technicalities when they threatened to expose the bribes.

When Miller reached the Corrido estate and advanced past the guarded gateway, he began taking long, deep breaths to calm himself. He would need to put on the performance of his life if he hoped to pull this off. What's more, if he were to succeed in getting his hands on the incriminating documents, he would have to consider using the gun in his hand for the first time in his life. He would have to kill Anthony Corrido.

As he expected, the black pickup wasn't parked in the driveway when he arrived at the mansion and parked. One of Corrido's underlings, a long-haired, moustachioed man in a Hawaiian print shirt and white shorts, approached the Mercedes as Miller was getting out.

'What's up, Commissioner? The boss won't be back for a while. I don't think he's expecting you, either.'

Miller circled around to the other side of the car and helped Sandy out. 'I wasn't expecting to come back out here, either, but I ran into a little problem, Nathan. Don't worry, I'll wait until Corrido gets here . . .'

THIRTY-TWO

Jesse continued to stare at the alley through his helmet visor. Norman's voice echoed his thoughts through the communication speakers. 'That's impossible. They can't have just disappeared. They had to go somewhere. Why don't you take a closer look at that –'

'Shhh,' Jesse hissed, interrupting Norman. 'Listen!'

From the direction of the large storm grating in front of Jesse, there came the distorted, echoing sound of high-pitched motors, growing fainter with each passing second.

'What was that?' Norman asked. 'Is that them?'

'Yeah, it's them all right.' Jesse activated the turret gun between his handlebars and took aim at the thick bars of the grating. Increasing the destructive force of the particle beam, he let loose with a blast that shook the bars until they were wrenched from their foundation. The other bikers might have had means to open the grating by remote control, but Jesse's way proved just as effective. In a matter of seconds, the opening to the city's sewer system was exposed and Jesse prepared to ride into the ominous concrete maw.

'Mach, what are you doing?'

'Playing a hunch,' Jesse told Norman. 'Stay tuned for more . . .'

Because there was an overall dampness to the walls of the sewers and a slick layer of water beneath his tyres, Jesse brought his speed up slowly. If this were a test run, he would have been wary of exceeding fifty miles an hour, but in his determination to get at the fleeing robbers he pushed past the safety limits, trusting his instincts to keep him and the bike in one piece.

'If you're going to drive like a maniac, at least flick on your brights,' Norman pleaded.

'I can't take my hands off the grips at this speed,' Jesse snapped. 'Now quit yakking in my ear and let me concentrate!'

'Mach, this is a two-man bike. I thought I already explained that to you. Look, I'm tracking your course and once you catch up to them, I'll let you know where you are.'

'Do that . . .'

Jesse raised his speed to sixty miles an hour.

Sixty-five.

Seventy.

Seventy-five.

Even through the insulation of his helmet, Jesse could hear the hiss of water flying out from beneath the tracks of his tyres. It was at least an inch deep, he figured.

'Hang tough, sweetheart.'

The tunnel curved in one direction then, a thousand feet later, in the other. Jesse held his speed and relied on the curvature of the sewer walls to allow him to corner the bike around the turns. He handled the first bend with no problem, but as he was whipping around the second, he suddenly saw a series of low-hanging cement buttresses reaching down so low that he stood a chance of catching them with his head. He reflexively veered sharply to his left, filling the tunnel with sparks as Street Hawk scraped against the cement walls. Jesse was able to keep the bike under control by forcing himself to keep his hand and foot off the brakes and relying on a shift of his body weight and an easing off on the accelerator. No sooner had he averted this near-disaster than he found himself coming up to a fork in the sewer. Fortunately, he gained enough ground on the thieves to be able to glimpse the rear tail-light of one of the bikers. He pursued it down the right leg of the sewer.

'I'm onto them, Norman. Where are we?'

'After that branch, if you maintain your present course, you should emerge somewhere around Carson and Imperial Highway . . . I think. I'm alerting the police, so be careful. Don't jeopardize my motorcycle.'

'I've got news for you, Norman. This bike's been in jeopardy since I first came across these yo-yos . . .'

There were a few inches of water in this part of the tunnel, and none of the three bikers were able to travel more than forty miles an hour. Street Hawk's advanced design and additional weight, however, allowed Jesse to draw even closer to his adversaries. He began to lock in on them with the monocle targeting system in his visor, but Norman abruptly urged him, 'Don't use your particle beam! The area's too confined!'

'What am I supposed to do, break out the lariat and lasso 'em?'

'Watch out, Jesse!'

One of the thieves was slowing down on his bike and turning to face Jesse. When he raised his arm and took aim with his wrist cannon, Jesse leaned forward and sped up, outracing the explosive dart that thundered off the wall behind him, ripping out a large section of the sewer wall.

'Here goes nothing,' Jesse murmured as he urged his bike onward until he was alongside the rear biker. Their bikes brushed against one another as water splashed up onto them. When the rider tried to get off a second shot, Jesse batted his arm away and the dart flew wild, exploding against the roof of the tunnel. Jesse continued to speed forward until he deliberately left himself sandwiched between the two robbers. The water around them was getting even deeper, forcing them to slow down further. Jesse's concentration was centred on the firing arm of the rider on his right. When he was sure the man was about to fire another dart, Jesse triggered Street Hawk's airfoils. His bike braked instantly and went into a slight skid as the other two bikes moved on. The dart intended for Jesse instead ploughed into the rear end of the other bike, rupturing the cocaine bags and knocking the cycle out of control. As a cloud of white dust began to fill the dank air of the tunnel, the second rider leapt from his bike seconds before it crashed into the sewer wall. He landed harshly in the water, but was still able to limp forward to where his comrade was waiting for him on the other bike. They rode off together, leaving behind the white fog that obscured even the infra-red capabilities of Jesse's visor.

'I can't see a thing, Norman!'

'Wait until it settles,' Norman recommended. 'And whatever you do, don't inhale...'

'But they're going to get away!'

'I don't think so,' Norman assured Jesse. 'It's been taken care of.'

The sewer gave way to a culvert through which the fleeing bikers rode, only to discover that the reason there was so much water in the tunnel was because a fire hydrant had been opened, flooding the basin. More than a dozen police officers stood around the periphery of the makeshift pool, barricading any possibility of escape for the cyclists.

As the thieves let their bike drop beneath them and threw their hands up in surrender, Anthony Corrido watched on from behind the wheel of his black pickup, which was parked behind an overgrown hedge half a block away. This time he wasn't gloating...

THIRTY-THREE

With Norman's help, Jesse was able to backtrack to the fork in the sewer and take the other leg to a point where he emerged to daylight behind an industrial complex near Washington Boulevard in the City of Commerce. From there, it was just a short drive to the downtown warehouse district. As Jesse pulled into Street Hawk's hideaway, he found Norman pacing about like a father who'd been waiting for his daughter to return home after her first date.

'What happened out there?' he howled shrilly as Jesse took off his helmet and climbed off the motorcycle. 'You endangered the entire mission when you first came on those bikers and just gawked at them until they headed off. If one of them had taken a potshot at you, you'd have been a sitting duck!'

Jesse tuned out Norman's rambling and walked past him toward the command module, asking, 'Did you see a black pickup on your monitor when they were making the hit? It would have been in the background, up around the overpass.'

'All I remember is seeing you freeze,' Norman jibed.

'Okay, so I spaced out for a minute. Get off my case already!'

'You don't space out on a three million dollar motorcycle, Mach!' Norman waved his arms in anguish, taking in the plethora of gadgetry around him. 'Do you realize what's at stake here? My dream . . . that's all!'

Jesse stopped and whirled around, causing Norman to nearly run into him. He met his cohort eyeball-to-eyeball and demanded, 'Norman, just answer my question. Did you see a black truck?'

The anger and urgency in Jesse's voice served to quell Norman's own tantrum. He backed away, realizing the reason for Jesse's concern. 'I don't remember,' he confessed, turning to the console before him. 'But if it was there, it's on tape.'

'Then cue it up. I want to see that tape!'

'Listen, Jesse. I know what you're up to, but I have to remind you that we have an agreement. This system is only to be used for specific test cases.'

'The hell with your test cases,' Jesse shot back. 'I need this information and you know it. Now, either you help me or you're going to have to find yourself another guinea pig. What's more, I'll blow the whistle on Street Hawk and –'

'All right, I'll pull the tape,' Norman conceded, scrambling his fingers across the keyboard that ran the console computers. 'This one time. But you have to promise me you'll turn over any information we get to the authorities. I won't endanger Operation Street Hawk for your personal vendetta.'

'Pull it,' Jesse said.

Once he had cued up the video image of Street Hawk's perspective of the flood channel, Norman sped up the tape, effectively recreating the blur of motion Jesse remembered experiencing as he was riding the bike in the grips of hyperthrust. When footage of city streets began to race across the screen, Norman slowed the tape, and soon he and Jesse were witnessing Jesse's arrival on the scene of the cocaine heist.

'Hold it!' Jesse called out, detecting what he was looking for. After Norman had stopped the tape, he said, 'Back it up, slowly.'

Norman was able to back up the tape frame by frame until he and Jesse simultaneously cried out. 'There it is!'

In the upper left-hand corner of the screen was the partially concealed black pickup. From the angle of the shot, it was impossible to see who the driver was, but the front end of the vehicle was more clearly in view.

'Can you enlarge the license plate?' Jesse asked.

'What do you think I am, a miracle worker?' Norman asked with a smug gleam in his eye. 'Just watch . . .'

Norman punched out a command and superimposed a grid

matte over the frozen frame. Singling out the small rectangle containing the licence plate, he next blew up that isolated section so that it filled the entire screen. Although the plate was marred by what looked like mud, both Jesse and Norman were clearly able to make out the numbers and letters stamped across it.

'Norman, I'll never say a bad thing about you again,' Jesse said, patting his partner on the back.

'Hah! Don't make promises you can't keep.' Norman quickly copied down the number and punched it into yet another computer. 'I'll check the DMV and see what we come up with.'

As Jesse stared over Norman's shoulder, the computer buzzed and clattered for a few seconds, then responded to Norman's inquiry by printing out Anthony Corrido's name and address on its viewing monitor.

'That's only a few miles from where Marty and I were cut down!' Jesse exclaimed. 'You're sure you punched in the right licence?'

'Positive,' Norman said, reaching for the phone. 'I'm going to call this in.'

'Before you do that,' Jesse said, 'could you let me into the weight room so I can change?'

'Where's your key card?'

Jesse grinned with embarrassment. 'In my pants pocket.'

Norman sighed and rolled his eyes as he led Jesse across to the smaller room. 'Why do I even ask? You know, my mother had this saying she was always using on my brother, who's as absent-minded as you are, Mach. She was always telling him that he'd lose his head if God hadn't screwed it . . . whaaaaa!'

Norman let out a pained yelp the moment he slipped his key card in the smaller room's lock. Jesse had grabbed him by the collar, and just when the door hissed open, Norman found himself shoved into the nearest Nautilis machine.

'Sorry, Norman,' Jesse called in as the door closed and he removed the key card.

'What are you doing?' Norman demanded.

'It's personal . . . and don't bother going through my pants because I have the other key card on me . . .'

Norman pounded helplessly on the plexiglass as Jesse walked out of view. 'Mach, open this door right now! Mach! Mach, do you hear me?'

Jesse heard Norman, but he wasn't about to let him out. Instead, he approached the command module console and pried open the lid of one of the control panels. He was familiar enough with rudimentary computer knowledge to know how to create the most snarl-ups with the least effort. After ripping loose a handful of wires and disconnecting a dozen crucial diodes, he left the immobilized console and strode over to Street Hawk. He donned his helmet and drowned out Norman's latest outburst with the throaty roar of the motorcycle's engine...

THIRTY-FOUR

Anthony Corrido's dark mood had changed from bad to worse by the time he returned to his desert mansion and found Commissioner Miller's Mercedes parked in the driveway. One of his nubile playmates spotted him and started scampering across the lawn toward him, only to shrink away at the mere sight of the scowl branded across Corrido's face. She tried to duck his gaze, but he'd already spotted her.

'If you so much as open your mouth I'm gonna rip that pretty tongue out of your face!' he threatened. 'Get out of my sight!'

The woman recoiled from Corrido's words as if she had been physically struck. She pulled her bathrobe tightly around her as she staggered away from Corrido, fear in her eyes. He stormed into his house and made his way to the study, where he found Miller and Nathan sipping drinks as they watched over Sandy. The Commissioner hadn't yet come up with a firm plan as to how he hoped to turn things to his favour, and when he noticed Corrido's expression, he instantly knew he was on thin ice.

'What's the matter?' Miller asked, setting down his drink. If the worst came to the worst, he wanted his gun hand free.

'It was a bust!' Corrido seethed as he went to the bar and quickly poured himself a shot of bourbon. He drowned it in one, then refilled the glass. 'Some guy on a custom bike came out of nowhere... my men couldn't lose him. You know anything about this, Miller?'

The Commissioner shook his head warily. 'No... I mean, there was some flak about some vigilante biker breaking up a robbery the other night, but it wasn't one of ours...'

Corrido's dark eyes bored into Sandy. 'Who the hell is this?'

'Her name is Sandy McCoy,' Miller said. 'She works for the department. She was asking about us at the body shop. Mach put her up to it. I didn't know what to do with her, so I brought her out –'

'So you brought her out here to dump in my lap!' Corrido muttered something under his breath and finished his drink, then slammed the empty glass down and turned to Nathan.

'Call the airport and make sure the plane's ready. Once Tanzia finds out the shipment was lost, he's gonna be on us for his money back and he's probably gonna want some heads on a platter. I want to be long gone by then, got it?'

Nathan bowed and drifted for the door. 'I'll get right on it!'

Corrido glanced back at Miller and Sandy. 'It might come in handy for us to have a hostage,' he thought out loud. Yanking out his gun, he drew a quick bead on Miller. 'For that matter, two hostages. Give me your piece, Commissioner.'

'What?'

'Don't play dumb with me! Your gun . . . take it out slowly with your fingertips and set it on the desk.' When Miller hesitated, Corrido pulled the hammer back on his own pistol. 'Now!'

Cursing himself for not having taken the incentive to use his gun earlier, the Commissioner reluctantly parted with his weapon, licking his lips, which had become suddenly dry. 'This is crazy, Corrido! You can't do this to me after all I've done helping you . . .'

'You just watch me!' Corrido shot back, snatching up Miller's pistol. 'Now, you and the missus better just sit still and keep your mouths shut. There's still an outside chance I won't have to blow you away . . .'

Sandy looked over at Miller and whispered, 'You should have listened to me.'

'The man said to shut up,' the Commissioner retorted bitterly.

Norman was on his knees before the exercise room door. He'd

already removed the plate covering the power box that worked the computer lock. After drawing in a deep breath, he carefully reached inside the box and disconnected several of the wires. He knew that if he crossed the wrong wires he could either short out the entire power supply to the building or send so many volts of electricity surging through his system that he would be dead with his hair smoking by the time he plopped to the ground. Ideally, he should have a pair of precision pliers to do what he was doing, but he had no choice but to risk his life if he wanted to get out of the room. Fortunately, he had slender fingers and was able to mate the two wires he needed to join. With an obedient hiss, the door rolled open.

'He'll pay for this!' Norman vowed as he bolted to the command console and slipped into the control seat. Some of the functions were still working, and he was able to cue up a subjective view of Street Hawk's perspective as Jesse entered the desert subdivision that housed Corrido's mansion.

'Mach, I want my motorcycle back immediately!' Norman bellowed as he put on his headset and flicked the necessary controls to put him in touch with Jesse. When he received no reply, Norman switched on another set of diodes, then realized the grim truth. 'What did you do with my controls! Mach . . . respond! Mach!' His face turning purple with rage, Norman removed the control panel that revealed the vandalism Jesse had wreaked on the wiring. 'You . . . you . . . saboteur!'

Jesse couldn't hear Norman's incensed raving. He raced down the main road of the subdivision, checking the street numbers painted on kerbs near each estate's main driveway. When he reached the gateway to Corrido's manor, Jesse applied Street Hawk's brakes and quickly readied the turret gun. When he saw that the remote-control video camera was sweeping its lens his way, he left the gun on its high setting and fired the crackling field of particle beams. The camera lens shattered almost immediately, but it took a longer concentration of the power force to pummel the gates until they fell aside like dry husks of corn in a stiff autumn breeze.

Once the way was clear, Jesse throttled his way up the drive, intent on confronting his long-sought enemy.

Commissioner Miller couldn't believe his good fortune. Corrido's safe was located in the wall behind his desk in the study, and he was hurriedly pulling out banded stacks of fifty and hundred dollar bills to stuff into a suitcase opened out on the desk. Miller had a clear view of the safe, and could see that in addition to the money, there were also a number of large files and envelopes stored in an upper shelf of the safe. He felt certain that the incriminating evidence against him was located amongst those papers. What was more, it seemed that Corrido was so involved in loading up on money that he was paying only scant attention to his would-be hostages. Miller's gun was lying on the corner of the desk, and the Commissioner felt that if he waited for just the right opportunity, he might be able to lunge for the weapon and have a chance to use it before Corrido could react.

Steady, he told himself. *Don't blow it by going for it too soon. If you misjudge him, he'll kill you on the spot. It has to be just the right moment.*

When he had emptied all the money from the safe, Corrido closed the lid of his suitcase, but it wouldn't clasp tight. Swearing to himself, Corrido set aside his own gun and leaned his full weight on the lid until he was able to snap the locks in place.

A split second before Commissioner Miller was about to make his move, an alarm over the study door suddenly clanged into life. Taken by surprise, Miller reflexively jerked to one side, nudging into Sandy and losing any semblance of the momentum he would have needed to pull off his last-ditch strategy.

Nathan swept back into the room seconds later, shouting over the alarm, 'The monitor's out! Somebody's busted into the grounds!'

'Damn, just what I need!' Corrido grabbed Miller's gun and tossed it to Nathan, then took his own gun along with the suitcase and charged out of the study. 'Whoever it is, I'm gonna take 'em out before they know what hit 'em!'

'Green one seven eight three five B . . . to red seven one four six C,' Norman murmured to himself as he tinkered with the damaged control panel. He pressed his lips together in concentrate as he made the connection . . . 'Blue six three two seven B . . . to yellow eight one ten K . . .' This time sparks flew and Norman quickly pulled the diode, correcting himself. 'No, yellow eight one *twelve* K . . .'

The connection was a clean one, and a signal light flashed on, confirming that Norman had re-established communication with Jesse. However, when he glanced up at the monitor screen, he refrained from saying anything, realizing in an instant that Jesse had his hands full.

The side door of the mansion burst open and Nathan rushed out, followed by another of Corrido's heavies, who toted a deadly looking M-203. As they fanned out and dropped into firing positions, Sandy and Commissioner Miller stepped out into the open, their hands in the air. Corrido was bringing up the rear, waving his gun back and forth at the spines of his hostages.

'Walk over to my truck!' he told them.

Just then Jesse burst into view, riding astride Street Hawk. Nathan and the other bodyguard immediately fired their weapons. A stream of hot lead scarred the driveway next to the motorcycle moments before the grenade fired from the M-203 exploded in front of Street Hawk.

'Stop!' Norman's voice crackled in Jesse's ear. 'Turn . . . do something!'

Jesse had to lay the bike down to avert the impact of the grenade, and Street Hawk skidded off the driveway and into the surrounding brush. Jesse dodged a round of bullets fired by Corrido and made for cover.

'Get him!' Corrido bade his underlings.

Like Miller, Sandy had been spending much of the past hour plotting a way to thwart the dismal fate she had stumbled into. She finally saw her opening. While Corrido and his two henchmen were all firing at Jesse, she lunged sharply to one side, clipping Commissioner Miller so hard he stumbled headlong into Corrido. During the moment's confusion, Sandy stepped out of her high heels and broke into a frantic dash around the side of the house, entering a plush garden area that extended all the way to Corrido's riding stables, two hundred yards away. A volley of gunfire ripped through the foliage around her, but all the shots missed their mark. For the time being, she was free . . .

THIRTY-FIVE

Scrambling on foot through the brush, Jesse found his helmet to be cumbersome, but he didn't want to stop long enough to remove it, figuring he was only a few seconds ahead of his pursuers. When he reached a gentle slope overgrown with bramble thickets, his racing suit helped to deflect the bite of prickles as he charged downhill toward the nearby stables. The men behind him cursed blue streaks as they encountered the feisty underbrush and were forced to slow down, although Nathan managed to catch a glimpse of Jesse heading for the stables.

The corral was deserted, and inside the stables Jesse could hear the nervous shuffling of horses nudging against their stalls. He circled around to the side door and let himself in. His visor automatically adjusted to the change in light, and his wide-angle perspective on the stable interior allowed him an advance warning when a fast-moving figure suddenly lunged out at him from the side, swinging a shovel in the direction of his head. Even with the added weight of the helmet, he was able to duck the blow.

'Wait!' he called out, recognizing Sandy. 'I'm on your side.'

Sandy slowly lowered the shovel, realizing she was looking at the bike rider who had provided the distraction that led to her freedom. She thought there was something familiar about the man's voice, but it was so distorted coming through the helmet she didn't guess it was Jesse. 'Who are you?' she asked.

'A friend,' Jesse assured her, moving back toward the door and opening it just enough to peer out.

'What's your name?'

'Ahh . . . Street Hawk,' Jesse murmured.

'Street Hawk.' Sandy frowned at the oddness of the name. 'I have to say, this has been one of the strangest days of my life.'

Jesse spotted Nathan clearing the brambles and heading for the stables with his companion close behind. Closing the door, he told Sandy, 'It isn't over yet . . . not by a long shot. The posse's just about to catch up with us . . .'

'What should we do?'

Jesse looked over his shoulder at the rest of the stable. There were at least twenty horses crowding the stalls, neighing and snorting at the presence of the two strangers. As he headed for the nearest stall, Jesse told Sandy, 'I think we should start rounding up some quick allies . . .'

'Look at these pants!' Nathan complained as he approached the stables. His white shorts were torn in several places and splotched with blood elsewhere from the scrapes and scratches he'd sustained during the chase. His legs looked as if they'd been flogged with barbed wire.

'Forget your damn pants,' the other man snapped, reloading his M-203. 'If we don't take care of things, your shorts are gonna look like they're off the rack compared to what Corrido's gonna do to us!'

'I wouldn't count on it,' Nathan said. 'While we're riskin' our necks, it wouldn't surprise me if he's already on his way outta here, along with our cut of the moola.'

When they reached the main doors of the stable, the two men paused. The one with the grenade launcher said, 'I'll wait here. You go around to the side door, then give a signal. Hopefully, we can box them in and kill two birds with one stone.' He patted his weapon.

'Some stone,' Nathan smirked.

Before the two men could split up, however, the main doors suddenly crashed open and half of the horses charged out, wild-eyed and reckless in celebration of their newfound freedom. The two gunmen were in the path of the stampede, and it was all they could do to avoid being trampled. Nathan quickly became separated from his companion and was knocked to the ground by a chestnut mare. He was mildly stunned by the blow, but he retained consciousness, and once the horses had all rushed past him, he slowly rose to his feet. As he was about to turn around, Jesse broadsided him with a force that made the horse's blow seem like a friendly pat on the back in comparison. Jesse followed Nathan to the ground and wrestled away his gun before knocking the man out by butting him in the head with his helmet.

'I knew there was a reason I was wearing this,' Jesse grumbled as he rose to his knees and brushed himself off.

'All right, pal!' Jesse felt something prodding him between his shoulder blades. He turned his head just enough to see the other bodyguard looming over him, pressing his M-203 against Jesse's spine. 'Drop that gun and get up, real slow-like...'

Jesse obeyed the man's orders, although he was secretly grinning behind his opaque visor. He had seen over the gunman's shoulder, to where Sandy was just about to cut loose with another swing of the shovel. This time her aim was true. With a dull groan, the thug with the grenade launcher sagged to his knees, then dropped forward, landing face-first in the dust next to Nathan.

'You should have yelled "fore",' Jesse teased as he stood up. 'Thanks.'

Sandy dropped the shovel, shocked at her behaviour. 'I don't know what came over me. Did you see that?' she gasped. 'I hit a man. I've never done that before.'

'You sure picked a nice time to start.' He took Nathan's gun from the dirt and handed it to her. 'Now, if you're lucky, you won't have to use this, too...'

THIRTY-SIX

The first thing Commissioner Miller heard when he regained consciousness was the sound of sirens screaming out in the desert, heading for the subdivision. As he blinked his eyes open and felt the sharp throbbing at the base of his skull, the tumble of events that had left him lying face-down on the driveway came back to him. After Sandy had shoved him into Corrido, Miller remembered flailing his arms in an attempt to keep his balance, only to succeed in tangling himself up with the drug dealer. Corrido had rammed an elbow or two into Miller's ribs, which still ached from the blows, then broken away and stood up. The last thing Miller recalled was Corrido glaring down at him and calling him some vile name that escaped him at the moment. There had been a glint of something, probably Corrido's gun coming his way, then nothing but a strange period of blackness invaded by pulses of rainbow-coloured sparks. Miller surmised that he had been knocked out with the butt of the gun and then left behind.

The whole flurry of thought took no more than the few seconds the Commissioner needed to sit up and shake the cobwebs from his head. He winced at the ache in his skull, but he had little time to dwell on past injuries, because his attention was soon occupied with avoiding yet another attempt on his life.

Corrido, behind the wheel of his black pickup, was barrelling down the driveway with a squeal of rubber, and Miller was directly in the path of the vehicle. He dived headlong to one side and the Land Rover hurtled past, missing him by inches. To be safe, Miller crawled on all fours into the brush lining the driveway and waited until he could no longer hear the truck. Then he picked himself up and hobbled across the asphalt towards his Mercedes. Before reaching the car, he was intercepted by the hysterical woman who had fled Corrido's insults an hour earlier.

'What's happening?' she wailed. 'I almost got shot! You have to help me before they kill me!'

'Get out of my way!' Miller said gruffly as he sidestepped the woman. 'Nobody's out to hurt you.'

'But –'

'But nothing!' Miller jerked his door open and yelled at the woman, 'Get inside and crawl under a bed or something!'

He locked the door behind him as he started up his engine, and when the woman continued to harass him through the tinted windows, he threw the Mercedes into reverse and cut the steering wheel sharply as he backed up, knocking her away. Shifting back into first, he raced down the driveway, swerving to avoid the sleek motorcycle that still lay on its side where Jesse had abandoned it.

It was a close race, but the police had beaten the Commissioner to the mansion entrance. Two patrol cars now barricaded the driveway so Miller had no chance of wriggling past them. A third police car raced past the mansion. As he bitterly turned off his ignition and prepared to surrender, Miller was barely able to make out Corrido's pickup roaring off down the main road, a few hundred yards ahead of the cops.

'Damn him,' he muttered. As a handful of officers approached his vehicle, Miller quickly started thinking up a cover story on the remote chance he could still talk his way out of trouble. He got out of the car and managed a grin as he faced the officers. 'Boy, am I glad to see you guys. This'll be the last time I try to play undercover cop by myself. I thought for sure I was going to be able to bust Corrido until –'

'Save your breath, Commissioner,' Officer Farnsworth said as he flashed a pair of handcuffs. 'We got a call from Sandy McCoy, so we know the whole story. You're under arrest . . .'

After he and Sandy had tracked down the phone in the stable,

Jesse had told her to call the station and stay put while he took off to see if he could prevent Corrido from getting away. Nathan was stirring, so he'd quickly found a length of rope and had tied both of Corrido's bodyguards together outside the stable, where Sandy could keep an eye on them through the window.

He heard sirens as he made his way back to the driveway, and he had to duck down behind the shrubs when Miller had driven by in the Mercedes. Once the way was clear and the howling woman had disappeared inside the mansion, Jesse lifted Street Hawk up and climbed back aboard. When he tried to start the engine, however, nothing happened.

'She's mine again,' Norman informed him through the helmet speakers. 'I just finished repairing the mess you made of my controls. I rewired the circuits for total override while I was at it. You don't go anywhere or do anything unless it's what I want, okay? Now be a good boy and bring Street Hawk in.'

'Norman, I have to finish this,' Jesse pleaded.

'That's out of the question.'

Jesse tried starting the bike again. Nothing. 'Hey, Norman, do you hear those sirens? This place is crawling with cops. Now either you let me have a go at Corrido or I give the police your motorcycle.'

'That's blackmail.'

'It's your choice, and I wouldn't spend that much time thinking about it, or it's going to be decided for you.'

There were a few seconds of tentative silence, then Street Hawk suddenly hummed to life and Norman's weary voice told Jesse, 'Do me one favour, Mach. Bring her back in one piece. Can you at least do that much for me?'

THIRTY-SEVEN

Commissioner Miller was being led into one of the police cars when Jesse powered down the driveway. Street Hawk had weathered its spill in fine form. When Jesse activated the vertical lift mechanism, the bike responded flawlessly, taking to the air over the bevy of cars choking the gateway to Corrido's mansion.

'What the hell . . .?' Farnsworth blurted as he saw the bike touch down on the main road and continue rolling in the direction the third police car had taken in its pursuit of Corrido. 'Somebody nab that hot dog once and for all!'

Officer Holt was in one of the patrol cars in the driveway, and he quickly backed up and then sounded his siren as he joined the chase.

Once he was out of the subdivision, Jesse slowly opened the throttle, picking up speed. The digital readout on his visor flashed the numbers in quick sequence – fifty . . . fifty-five . . . sixty . . . sixty-five . . . seventy . . .

'Okay, Mach,' Norman reported. 'I've run all the troubleshooting tests and everything checks out okay. The frame's intact and you should be able to push it without picking up any vibration. If you do, though, pull back.'

'Got it, Norman.' Jesse banked around a corner and found himself on a straightaway that cut through the middle of the desert. Out ahead of him, he could see the flashing lights of the patrol car chasing Corrido. Behind him, the other cruiser was holding its pace, keeping up with him.

'Mother, may I take one giant step forward?' he murmured as he goosed the throttle. Street Hawk jolted forward, and within a matter of seconds Jesse was travelling at more than a hundred miles an hour, gaining ground on those in front of him while he left Officer Holt falling way behind.

At a point halfway across the barren plain, Corrido abandoned the highway in favour of a rugged dirt road that wound up into the foothills surrounding the desert. The Land Rover kicked up a billowing cloud of dust as Corrido took the corner wide rather than slowing down, as the police car had to do. There was an immediate bend in the road, curving around a mesquite-covered hill. Corrido took the turn wide as well, and was subsequently able to avoid colliding with a stalled field truck that was straddling most of both lanes in the road. The pickup's monstrous tyres found a firm footing on the soft dirt of the shoulder, keeping Corrido from sliding down the embankment as he drove past the other truck and got back on the road. The police cruiser wasn't so fortunate, however. Trying to pick up speed as he rounded the corner, the driver slammed on his brakes at the sight of the stalled truck, and the patrol car fishtailed sideways into the eight-wheeled roadblock.

When Street Hawk whipped around the corner, Jesse quickly triggered his vertical lift at the same time Norman was shouting in his ear, 'Watch it! Jump!'

'Thanks, Norman.'

As Street Hawk landed and continued its forward motion, Norman couldn't help but gush, 'Perfect! You're handling it like a champ, Mach! Now, go!'

'You sound pretty excited there, Norman,' Jesse joked as he sped up. 'I could almost swear you were cheering me on instead of putting me down!'

'Okay, okay, so I over-reacted!' Norman confessed. 'Look, we'll never get a better chance to show off what Street Hawk can do, so go for it!'

Riding with Corrido in the pickup truck was yet another of his flunkies, a bleach-blond bruiser named Alfred, who had been keeping an eye on the pursuing police car, ready to fire at it with an Uzi submachine gun if it drew too close. After they had circumvented the field truck and he'd witnessed the collision of the cruiser in the rear-view mirror, Alfred relaxed slightly and turned to Corrido. 'So much for the heat. Now we just have to make it to the airfield.'

'Yeah, how about... what in blazes?' Corrido spotted a blur in his side-view mirror and soon realized it was Jesse. 'Where the hell did he come from?'

Alfred stuck his head out the window for a better look. 'It's that same guy who –'

'I know that, dammit! Take him out, Alfred!'

'Sure thing.' Alfred reached behind him and slid open the cab windows leading to the back shell of the truck. As Corrido raced on, he carefully wriggled through the opening, then pulled his Uzi in after him and crept to the rear of the shell and prepared to throw open the door so he could have a clear shot at Jesse.

Jesse was lining up his own clear shot through the monocle targeting system built into his visor. Once the circle was centred on the pickup, he prepared to fire a particle beam. When he triggered the gun, however, nothing happened.

'Mach,' Norman relayed the bad news. 'I'm getting a malfunction warning on your weapon system. Something must have jarred –'

Norman's transmission suddenly was cut off, and Jesse heard the electrical popping of circuits shorting inside his helmet.

'Norman? Norman, are you there?'

When there was no response, Jesse guessed that he had been cut off from any contact with the master control module. No doubt the impact of his landing after two vertical lift manoeuvres had fouled up part of his intercom linking. Once again, Street Hawk was on its own, with only Jesse's expertise to guide it. Jesse wasn't altogther disappointed. The malfunction hadn't apparently affected the mechanical running of the bike, and when he revved his throttle, he gained considerable ground on the pickup.

Street Hawk was less then fifty feet away from the Land Rover and still gaining when the tailgate suddenly flapped open and Alfred leaned out, opening fire with his Uzi. Jesse veered his bike sharply to one side, coming within inches of the road's shoulder as he avoided the stream of lethal lead. With his left hand, he quickly jimmied the bike's handle grip, dislodging the Dum-Dum gun Norman had demonstrated to him during the middle stages of his training. As he guided the bike closer to the truck, Jesse raised the gun and fired directly at Alfred.

The rubber bullet that charged out of the gun had been tested by Norman as part of a study to develop an effective weapon for use in riot-control. It was designed to immobilize someone without inflicting a skin-breaking wound, and it lived up to its reputation by striking Alfred so hard in the chest he dropped his machine gun and fell off balance out of the speeding truck. Jesse weaved around the falling figure and continued in pursuit of Corrido. Alfred bounced harshly off the pavement and landed on the shoulder of the road, battered and bruised but still alive.

Corrido saw Alfred fall out of the truck, but he lost sight of Street Hawk for several seconds as Jesse tailed him in the pickup's blind spot. When Corrido changed his speed abruptly and caught a glimpse of Jesse's position, he cranked his steering wheel sharply to the right, leaving the road. Jesse stayed with him, rising slightly on the pegs of his bike to buffer the rough terrain of the road's shoulder. For several hundred yards they raced side by side, with Corrido unable to edge Jesse any further off the shoulder for fear of losing control of his own vehicle.

Corrido was so involved with Jesse that he wasn't paying full attention to the way before him. Soon he was racing headlong toward a billboard poster by the side of the road. Clamping both hands on the wheel, he braced himself and drove up a sharp pitch in the shoulder, making his track airborne so that at the same time Jesse was leaning his bike under the sign, Corrido was crashing through it, splintering the thin wood with ease. He retained control of the vehicle, and when it nosed down onto the soft dirt of the shoulder, he was able to slow to a stop well before the sloping embankment.

Jesse was now more than four dozen yards ahead of the pickup. He idled his bike and looked over his shoulder, flipping up his visor long enough to give Corrido a chance to see who it was that had disrupted his plans for escape.

'Mach!' Corrido roared, fuelled with a fresh jolt of rage. 'I should have known!'

When Jesse lowered his visor and drove down the embankment leading back to the flatlands, Corrido jammed his gearbox, putting the truck into four-wheel drive as he vehemently seized the role of chaser. With Street Hawk now in its off-road suspension mode, both vehicles were in their own element. They sped across the landscape with seeming abandon. Gravel and topsoil spat out from under tyre treads; engines whined with high RPMS when either the bike or truck made a sharp turn or began to climb a sudden rise in the terrain.

The lay of the land struck Jesse as vaguely familiar, and when he spotted the electrical wires stretching across the desert in the distance, he knew he was in the vicinity of the old airfield. Relying on other landmarks that he recalled from that fateful day when he had almost lost his life, Jesse led Corrido in the direction of the tarmac, which soon came into view. To Jesse's surprise, the same plane that had almost run him down weeks ago was now idling on the landing track, with a few men standing around it. He quickly changed course, making it look to Corrido as if he was hoping to drop out of view in the overgrown maze of sagebrush and chapparal. Corrido took the bait and continued with the chase rather than heading for the plane.

'You cheated death once on me, Mach!' Corrido growled as he floored the accelerator and crashed through the brush. 'It won't happen again!' He was obsessed with his quest and gave no thought to letting Jesse escape, even when his getaway plane was ready and waiting for him. He was familiar with the nature of the foliage in this area, and with his bulkier machine, he didn't have to worry as much as Jesse about running into something that might not give under the force of a collision. As such, he was able to pull up close to Jesse as they approached the gorge. Forty feet away . . . thirty-five . . . thirty . . . twenty-five . . .

Jesse knew he was losing ground to Corrido, but he did

little to change the situation. Even when he cleared the brush and was racing across bare desert toward the spot where his friend Marty had lost his life, Jesse refused to open his throttle further. Corrido took advantage of Jesse's apparent blunder and floored his own accelerator, closing the final gap between the two vehicles and ramming Street Hawk's rear end. Jesse kept the bike under control and finally put on a burst of speed to pull ahead, prompting Corrido to follow suit.

Jesse knew his life depended on both his memory and his timing. Veering slightly to his right, he set a course that headed directly for the edge of the gorge and brought his speed up to more than ninety miles an hour. In his rear-view mirror, he saw that Corrido was still matching his pace, if not surpassing it.

'This thing better still work,' Jesse whispered to himself as he suddenly put the bike into vertical lift at the same time he was jamming on the airfoil braking system.

As Norman had predicted, the result of his manoeuvre was that Street Hawk launched itself into an incredible forward loop that rivalled anything ever attempted by an aerial stunt pilot at an airshow during the heydey of daredevil flying. In this case, Jesse's only audience was Anthony Corrido, and the drug dealer was stunned with disbelief at what he was seeing.

When Jesse completed his roll and made a perfect pinpoint landing directly behind the pickup, Corrido looked over his shoulder, his eyes wide with shock. By the time he realized that Jesse had deliberately lured him to the edge of the gorge before going into the roll, it was too late for Corrido to avoid the fate he had imposed upon Marty Walsh at this same precipice several weeks before. He pumped at his brakes, but by then the pickup had already raced too close to the cliff, and Corrido let out a scream that lasted as long as it took the truck to tumble down the sheer facing of the gorge and dash itself into a twisted heap on the jagged boulders at the bottom of the precipice.

Jesse rode to the edge of the gorge and raised his visor as he looked down at the remains of the truck. Corrido was hanging halfway out of the pickup, unmoving.

'It's over,' he muttered to himself, lowering the visor and turning his bike away from the dropoff. Over the airstrip, a pair of Highway Patrol cruisers had arrived and were closing in on Corrido's private plane. Jesse wasn't interested in showing himself or the bike to the authorities any longer. Staying close to the edge of the gorge, he rode off, heading west toward the sunset...

EPILOGUE

Although Norman had been cut off from communicating with Jesse or assisting in the operation of Street Hawk during the final chase, the motorcycle's monitors had continued to function. When Jesse returned to Street Hawk's operational headquarters that evening, he found Norman in a euphoric daze.

'I can't believe you did it! It's . . . incomprehensible!'

'What are you talking about?' Jesse asked as he climbed off the bike and removed his helmet. 'Corrido? Well, I couldn't help it, it was just something that I had to do . . . that scumbag had it coming to him!'

'That's not what I mean,' Norman retorted, waving for Jesse to join him at the master control module. 'I'm talking about *this*!!'

Jesse glanced at the video screen, where the footage of his last-ditch manoeuvre played in a slow, dream-like motion. From the subjective perspective of the camera, there was a dizzying view of the ground falling away, only to be replaced by a few moments of azure, cloud-streaked sky, and then back to earth again, with a view of the black pick up brodying to one side seconds before it toppled over the edge of the precipice.

'That was a full forward loop, Mach! Do you realize that?'

'I was there, Norman, remember?' Jesse said casually, trying to downplay the feat.

'I mean, it's been done before, but only on a loop track. You did it in midair, for crying out loud! One second I was sure that the past four years of my life were going to end up in a wrecked heap, and the next thing I know you've pulled the stunt of a lifetime without even losing your balance on landing!'

Jesse grinned and flashed a thumbs-up signal. 'I guess maybe your boss had me pegged when he said I had the right stuff, huh?'

Norman ignored Jesse's boast and wandered away from the console to inspect Street Hawk. It only took him a few seconds to pinpoint the source of the bike's malfunction. 'Ah, this is nothing major. A little design change and I can have this fixed right up.'

Jesse yawned as he slipped his card key into the lock of the exercise room. 'You go ahead, Norman. I'm beat. I think I'm gonna change and go home . . . Oh, by the way, Norman, I'm sorry about locking you up in here. I hope you understand.'

Norman looked over his shoulder, offering a stern gaze. 'I'm willing to let that pass this time, Mach. If it happens again, though, there's going to be trouble. This is a team operation. I hope I don't have to mention that again.'

'Right.'

The day's fatigue was catching up with him quickly, and by the time Jesse had left the warehouse and driven his Mustang home, he was having trouble keeping his eyes open. Trudging up to his apartment, he collapsed on his living room sofa and slipped into a deep slumber. He had a number of dreams throughout the night, filled with sensations of flight and images of Anthony Corrido's black pickup chasing him across vast terrains, but he nonetheless slept soundly enough to feel revitalized when he woke up. He also realized he had overslept. As he went to his phone to notify the station he would be late for work, he saw there were messages on his answer phone. All of them were from Sandy, inquiring worriedly as to his whereabouts and telling him briefly about the apprehension of Commissioner Miller and the death of Anthony Corrido, both due to the intervention of the mysterious biker called Street Hawk.

'If she only knew,' Jesse mused as he dialled the station. He got Freddie on the line and asked him to pass along a message to Sandy that he had been sidetracked on a false lead the previous day and had just gotten back into town moments ago. He then took a quick shower and grabbed a few pieces of fruit from the refrigerator on his way out of the door.

Commander Altobelli was enduring yet another press conference when Jesse punched in for work and took over Freddie's post at the doorway with the usual press handouts. Sandy was up on stage next to Altobelli, and she and Jesse traded glances. Her face was torn between relief and agitation. Jesse smiled tightly, then looked away from her and focused on Altobelli's ordeal at the podium.

'... and because of the nature of the investigation of Commissioner Miller's involvement in this case, we have no comment at this time other than the facts I've just presented.'

'You still haven't told us about the guy on the motorcycle,' a reporter called out from the throng of newsmen crowding the room. 'From what little we've heard, it sounds like the same guy who –'

'No comment!' Altobelli bellowed. Behind the podium, he started unwrapping an antacid tablet.

'Is it true that this guy's bike is capable of vaulting and doing other stunts that have never been –'

'No comment!!'

Sandy leaned close to Altobelli and whispered in his ear. 'If you stonewall them too much, they're going to start speculating and it's apt to turn out worse than if you spoonfeed them a few facts.'

Altobelli cupped his hand over the microphone and grumbled, 'I hate this!'

'Come on, chief, you can do better than that,' a voice wheedled from the back of the crowd.

The Commander sighed, then divulged, 'The unidentified motorcycle rider who participated in the incident at the liquor store the other evening was, as far as we know, the same biker who was at the scene of the cocaine heist and the altercation with the alleged dealers out in the desert. When the suspect was approached for questioning, he fled. Now, if you want my honest opinion, I think this guy has had his fill of joyriding and it's the last we'll ever see of him ... thank you, and good day ...'

Altobelli turned off his microphone and left the podium.

Deep in his heart, he didn't really believe his last remark.

Neither did Jesse Mach...